HOME AGAIN

George MacDonald

edited by
Dan Hamilton

VICTOR BOOKS ®

A DIVISION OF SCRIPTURE PRESS PUBLICATIONS INC.
USA CANADA ENGLAND

Home Again was first published in England in 1887.

Library of Congress Catalog Card Number: 88-60211
ISBN: 0-89693-464-0

© 1988 by Dan Hamilton
Printed in the United States of America

Cover Illustration: James Tennison

VICTOR BOOKS
A division of Scripture Press Publications, Inc.
Wheaton, Illinois 60187

Contents.

Introduction ..../7

Chapter 1 ....The Parlor/9
Chapter 2 .... The Arbor/13
Chapter 3 ....A Pennyworth of Thinking/16
Chapter 4 .... Thinks and Things/21
Chapter 5 ....Flutterbies/23
Chapter 6 .... A Father's Gift/27
Chapter 7 .... London/30
Chapter 8 .... The Ruin of Dreams/34
Chapter 9 .... The Field Battery/37
Chapter 10 ....Flattery/40
Chapter 11 .... By Arrangement/43
Chapter 12 .... The Round of the World/46
Chapter 13 ....The Song/49
Chapter 14 .... The Face of Lufa/53
Chapter 15 .... Home Is Where the Heart Is?/57
Chapter 16 ....A Midnight Review/61
Chapter 17 ....A Pale Reflection/65
Chapter 18 ....A Ride Together/70
Chapter 19 .... Walter's Firstborn/74
Chapter 20 ....A Blossom in Winter/77
Chapter 21 ....The Bodiless/82
Chapter 22 .... The Soulless/85
Chapter 23 .... The Last Ride?/91
Chapter 24 .... The Summerhouse/95
Chapter 25 ....Into the Park/101

Chapter 26...The Drawing Room/104
Chapter 27...A Midnight Encounter/109
Chapter 28... The Slow Dawn/115
Chapter 29..A Hard Letter/122
Chapter 30..A Sudden Journey/129
Chapter 31...Doing and Dreaming/134
Chapter 32.................................... Duties and Defiance/137
Chapter 33... Molly's Wings/140
Chapter 34..Molly's Words/145
Chapter 35..Molly's Wisdom/149
Chapter 36................................The Last, But Not the End/156

Editor's Afterword 159

Introduction.

George MacDonald (1824-1905), a Scottish preacher, poet, novelist, fantasist, expositor, and public figure, is most well known today for his children's books—*At the Back of the North Wind, The Princess and the Goblin, The Princess and Curdie,* and his fantasies *Lilith* and *Phantastes.*

But his fame is based on far more than his fantasies. His lifetime output of more than fifty popular books placed him in the same literary realm as Charles Dickens, Wilkie Collins, William Thackeray, and Thomas Carlyle. He numbered among his friends and acquaintances Lewis Carroll, Mark Twain, Lady Byron, and John Ruskin.

Among his later admirers were G.K. Chesterton, W.H. Auden, and C.S. Lewis. MacDonald's fantasy *Phantastes* was a turning point in Lewis' conversion; Lewis acknowledged MacDonald as his spiritual master, and declared that he had never written a book without quoting from MacDonald.

Chapter 1.

THE PARLOR

Dimly visible in the July dusk, two elderly people sat in the old-fashioned best room of a farmhouse, breathing the fragrance which unseen roses sent through the twilight and into the open window.

To the old man, Richard Colman, the roses brought too much sadness to be welcome, for they seemed to issue from the grave of his vanished youth. He was not by nature a sad man, but he was one who had found the past more delightful than the present, and had not left his first loves. The twilight of his years had crept upon him and was deepening, and he felt his youth slowly withering under their fallen leaves. With more education, and perhaps more receptivity than most farmers, he had married a woman he fervently loved, whose rare and truthful nature had developed the delicate flower of moral and social refinement; and her influence upon him had been of the eternal sort. While many of their neighbors were vying with each other in the effort to dress and dwell and live up to their notion of gentility, Richard and his wife had never troubled themselves about fashion, but had each sought to please the taste of the other, and to cultivate their own. Perhaps now as he sat thus silent in the twilight, he was holding closer converse than he knew, or than any of us can know, with one who seemed to have vanished from all this side of things, who had fallen asleep for the final time—who had *died*, as the world persists in calling it. The heart of her husband clung to what people would call

9

her memory; I prefer to call it *her*.

The old woman beside him was scarcely conscious of the scent, for she did not believe in roses; she believed mainly in mahogany, linen, and hams, and it was she who tore the rose-scented hush with her strident cicada-like shrilling.

"Richard, that son of yours will come to no good! You may take my word for it!"

Mr. Colman made no answer, and the dusky, sweet-smelling waves of the silence closed over the laceration.

"I am well aware my opinion is of no value in your eyes, Richard," she continued, "but that does not absolve me from the duty of stating it. If you allow him to go on as he is, Walter will never eat bread of his own earning!"

The father thought, but nowise said, "There are many who do, and yet don't come to much!"

"What do you mean to make of him?" persisted Miss Hancock, the half sister of his wife, the *a* in whose name Walter said ought to have been an *e*.

"Whatever he is able to make of himself. He must have the main hand in it, whatever it be," answered Mr. Colman.

"It is time twice over he had set about something! You let him go on dawdling and dawdling without even making up his mind whether or not he ought to do anything! Take my word for it, Richard—you'll have him on your hands till the day of your death!"

The father did not reply that he could wish nothing better, that the threat was more than he could hope for. He did not want to provoke his sister-in-law, and he knew there was a shadow of reason in what she said, though even perfect reason could not have sweetened the mode in which she said it. Nothing could make up for the total absence of sympathy in her utterance of any modicum of truth she was capable of uttering. She was a very dusty woman, and never more dusty than when she fought against dust as in a warfare worthy of all a woman's energies. Because she had not a spark of Mary in her, she imagined herself a Martha. She was true as steel to the interests of those in whose lives she was involved, but only in their dusty interests, not those which make man worth God's trouble. She was a vessel of clay in an outbuilding of the temple, and took on her the airs—not of gold, for gold has no airs—but of clay imagining itself gold, and all the golden vessels nothing but clay.

"I put it to you, Richard," she went on, "whether good ever came of reading poetry and falling asleep under haystacks! He actually writes poetry, and we all know what *that* leads to!"

"Do we?" ventured her brother-in-law. "King David wrote poetry!"

"Richard, don't garble! I will not have you garble! You know what I mean as well as I do myself! And you know as well as I do what comes of writing poetry! That friend of Walter who borrowed ten pounds of you—that man Sullivan—did he ever pay it to you?"

"He did, Ann."

"You didn't tell *me!*"

"I did not want to disappoint you!" replied Richard, with a stream of sarcasm she did not feel.

"It was worth telling!" she returned.

"I did not think so. Not everybody sticks to a banknote like a snail to a wall! I returned him the money."

"Returned him the money!"

"Yes."

"Made him a present of *ten pounds?*"

"Why not?"

"Why then?"

"I had more reasons than one."

"And no call to explain them! It was just like you to throw away your hard earnings on a fellow that would never earn anything for himself! As if one such wasn't enough to take all you'd got!"

"How could he send back the money if that had been the case? He proved himself what I believed him, ready and willing to work! The money went for a fellow's bread and cheese, and what better money's worth would you have?"

"You may someday want the bread and cheese for yourself!"

"One stomach is as good as another."

"It never was and never will be any use talking to some people," concluded Ann, in the same tone she began with, for she seldom lost her temper—though no one would have much minded her losing it, it was so little worth keeping. Rarely angry, she was always disagreeable. The good that was in her had

11

no flower, but bore its fruit in the shape of good food, clean linen, mended socks, and suchlike, without any blossom of sweet companionship to make life pleasant.

Aunt Ann would have been quite justified in looking on poetry with contempt, had it been what she imagined. Like many others, she held decided opinions concerning things of which her idea nowise corresponded with the things themselves.

Chapter 2.

THE ARBOR

While the elders thus conversed in the dusky drawing room, where the smell of the old roses almost overpowered the new, another couple sat in a little homely bower in the garden. It was Walter and his rather distant cousin, Molly Wentworth; for fifteen years they had been as brother and sister. Their fathers had been great friends, and when Molly's parents died in India, Richard Colman took the little orphan home—much to the joy of his wife, who had often longed for a daughter to perfect the family ideal. The more motherly a woman is, the nearer will the child of another satisfy the necessities of her motherhood. Mrs. Colman could not have said which child she loved best.

Over the still summer garden rested a weight of peace. It was a night to the very mind of the fastidious, twilight-loving bat flitting about, coming and going like a thought we cannot help. Most of Walter's thoughts came and went thus. He had not yet learned to think; he was hardly more than a medium in which thought came and went. Yet when a thought seemed worth anything, he always gave himself the credit for it—as if a man were author of his own thoughts anymore than of his own existence! A man can but so live with the life given him that this or that kind of thought shall call on him, and to this or that kind he shall not be at home. Walter was only at that early stage of development where a man is in love with what he calls his own thoughts.

Even in the dark of the summerhouse one might have seen

that he was pale, and might have suspected him handsome. In the daylight his gray eyes might almost seem the source of his paleness. His features were well marked though delicate, and had a notable look of distinction. He was above the middle height, and slender; he had a wide forehead and a small, pale moustache on an otherwise smooth face. His mouth was his least interesting feature; it had great mobility, but when at rest, little shape and no attraction. For this, however, his smile made considerable amends.

The girl was dark, with a clear, pure complexion and fine-grained skin. If at first she gave the impression of delicacy, it soon changed into one of compressed life, of latent power. The dusk had become night now, and her eyes were too dark to appear—they sank into it, and were as the unseen soul of the dark; while her mouth, rather large and exquisitely shaped with the curve of a strong bow, seemed as often as she smiled to make a pale window in the blackness. Her hair came rather low down the steep of her forehead, and, with the strength of her chin, made her face look rounder than seemed fitting.

They sat for a time as silent as the night that enfolded them. They were not lovers, though they loved each other perhaps more than either knew. They were watching to see the moon rise at the head of the valley, on one of whose high, sloping sides they sat.

The moon kept her tryst, and revealed a loveliness beyond what the day had to show. She looked upon a wide valley that gleamed with the windings of a river. She brightened the river, and dimmed in the houses and the cottages the lights with which the opposite hill sparkled like a celestial lamp. She did her lovely work from the heavens, her poor mirror work—all she was fit for now, affording fit room, atmosphere, and medium to young imaginations unable yet to spread their wings in the sunlight, and believe what lies hid in the light of the workaday world. Nor was what she showed the less true for what lay unshown in shrouded antagonism, though the vulgar cry for the supposed real would bury in deepest grave every eternal fact. This is the cry, "Not this man, but Barabbas!"

For the day would reveal a river stained with loathsome refuse, and rich gardens on hillsides mantled in sooty smoke and evil-smelling vapors, sent up from a valley where men, like gnomes, toiled and caused to toil too eagerly. What would one think of a housekeeper so intent upon saving that she could waste no time on beauty or cleanliness? How many who would storm, if they came home to an untidy house, yet feel no shadow of uneasiness that they have all day been defiling the house of the Father, nor at night lift a hand to cleanse it? Such men regard others as fools, whose joy a foul river can poison; yet, as soon as they have by pollution gathered and saved their god, they make haste to depart from the spot they have ruined! Oh, for an invasion of indignant ghosts, to drive from the old places the generation that dishonors the ancient earth! The sun shows all their disfiguring, but the friendly night comes at length to hide her disgrace; and once that is well hidden, the brooding moon slowly ascends to unveil her beauty.

There was a thriving town full of awful chimneys in the valley, and the clouds that rose from it ascended above the Colman farm to the great moor which stretched miles and miles beyond it. In the autumn sun its low forest of heather burned purple; in the pale winter it lay white under snow and frost; but through all the years, winds would blow across it the dull smell of the smoke from below. Had such a fume risen to the earthly paradise, Dante would have imagined his purgatory sinking into hell.

On all this inferno the night had sunk like a foretaste of cleansing death. The fires lay smoldering like poor, hopeless devils, desirous of sleep. The world was merged in a tidal wave from the ocean of hope, and seemed to heave a restful sigh under its cooling renovation.

Chapter 3.

A PENNYWORTH OF THINKING

"A penny for your thoughts, Walter!" said the girl after a long silence, in which the night seemed at length to clasp her too closely.

"Your penny, then! I was thinking how wild and sweet the dark wind would be, blowing up there among the ringing bells of the heather."

"You shall have the penny. I will pay you with your own coin. I keep all the pennies I win of you. What do you do with those you win of me?"

"Oh, I don't know. I take them because you insist on paying your bets, but—"

"Debts, you mean, Walter! You know I never bet, even in fun! I hate taking things for nothing! I wouldn't do it!"

"Then what are you making me do now?"

"Take a penny for the thought I bought of you for a penny. That's fair trade, not gambling. And your thought tonight is well worth a penny. For a moment I felt the very wind on the moor."

"I'm afraid I shan't get a penny a thought in London!"

"Then you *are* going to London, Walter?"

"Yes, indeed! What else? What is a man to do here?"

"What is a man to do there?"

"Make his way in the world."

"But, Walter, please let me understand! Indeed, I don't want to be disagreeable! What do you wish to make your way to?"

"To such a position as—" Here he stopped, unsure.

"You mean to fame and honor and riches, don't you, Walter?" ventured Molly.

"No, not riches. Did you ever hear of a poet and riches in the same breath?"

"Oh, yes, I have! Though somehow they don't seem to go together comfortably. If a poet is rich, he ought to show he couldn't help it."

"Suppose he was made a lord, where would he then be without money?"

"If to be a lord one must be rich, he ought never to wish to be a lord. But you do not want to be either lord or millionaire, Walter, do you?"

"I hope I know better!"

"Where does the way you speak of lead then, Walter? To fame?"

"If it does, what would you have to say against it? Even Milton calls it, 'That last infirmity of noble mind'!"

"But he calls it an infirmity, and such a bad infirmity, apparently, that it is the hardest of all to get rid of!"

The fact was that Walter wanted to be—and thought he was—a poet, but it was far from certain. He feared it might not be so, and therefore greatly desired the verdict of men in his favor, if but for his own satisfaction. Fame was precious to him, for determining his position in the world of letters—his kingdom of heaven. Well read, he had not used his reading practically enough to perceive that the praise of one generation may be the contempt of another, perhaps of the very next, so that the repute of his time could assure him of nothing. He did not know the worthlessness of the opinion that either grants or withholds fame.

He looked through the dark at his cousin, thinking, "What sets her talking of such things? How can a girl understand a man with his career before him?"

She read him through the night and his silence. "I know what you are thinking, Walter!" she said. "You are thinking women can't think. But I should be ashamed not to have common sense, and I cannot see the sense of doing anything for the praise that can help nothing and settle nothing."

"Why then should all men have the desire for it?"

"That they may get rid of it. Why do all men have vanity? Where would the world be on the way to now, if Jesus Christ had sought the praise of men?"

"But He has it!"

"Not much of it yet, I suspect. He does not care for the praise that comes before obedience! That's what I have heard your father say."

"I never heard him."

"I have heard him say it often. What could Jesus care for the praise of one whose object in life was the praise of men?"

Walter had not lost the reverence of his childhood. He believed himself to have high ideals, and felt that a man must be upright or lose his life. So strongly did he feel it, that he imagined himself therefore upright, and incapable of a dishonest or mean thing. He had never done—never could do, he thought—anything unfair. But to what Molly said, he had no answer. What he half thought in his silence was something like this—that Jesus Christ was not the *type* of manhood, but a man by Himself who came to do a certain work; that it was both absurd and irreverent to talk as if other men had to do as He did, to think and feel like Him; that He was so high above the world He could not care for its fame, while to mere man its praises must be dear. Nor did Walter make any right distinction between the commendation of understanding men who know the thing they praise, and the empty voice of the unwise many.

In a word, Walter thought—without knowing he did—that Jesus Christ was not a man.

"I think Molly," he said, "we had better avoid the danger of irreverence."

For the sake of his poor reverence he would frustrate the mission of the Son of God, and justify himself in refusing the judgment of Jesus!

"I know you think kindly of me, Molly," he went on, "and I should be sorry to have you misunderstand me; but surely a man should not require religion to make him honest. I scorn the notion. A man must be just and true because he is a man! Surely a man may keep clear of the thing he loathes! For my own honor," he added, with a curl of his lip, "I shall at least do nothing disgraceful, however short I may fall of the angelic."

"I doubt," murmured Molly, "whether a man is a man until

he knows God."

But Walter, if he heard the words, neither needed nor answered them. He was far from understanding the absurdity of doing right from the love of self.

He was no hypocrite, for he did turn from what seemed to be degrading; but there were degrading things which he did not see to be such, things on which some men, to whom he did not yet look up, would have looked down. Also there was that in his effort to sustain his self-respect which was far from pure; he despised such as had failed, and to despised the human because it has fallen is to fall from the human. He had done many little things he ought to be—and one day must be, but as yet felt no occasion to be—ashamed of. So long as they did not trouble him, they seemed nowhere.

Many a youth starts in life as Walter did, possessed with the vague idea that he is a most precious specimen of pure and honorable humanity. It comes of self-ignorance, and a low ideal taken for a high one. Such are mainly among the well behaved, and never doubt themselves a prize for any woman. They color their notion of themselves with their ideal, and then mistake the one for the other. The mass of weaknesses and conceits that compose their being they compress into their ideal mold of man, and then regard the shape as their own. What composes it they do not heed.

No man, however, could look in the refined face of Walter Colman and imagine him cherishing sordid views of life. Asked what of all things he most admired, he might truly answer, "The imaginative intellect." He was a fledgling poet. He worshiped what he called thoughts, would rave about a thought in the abstract, and turn aside after an uncaught idea. When a concrete thinkable one fell to him, he was jubilant over the isolated thing, but its value had nothing to do with his joy. He would stand wrapped in the delight of what he counted its beauty, and yet more in the delight that his was the mind that had generated such a meteor! To be able to think pretty things was to him a gigantic distinction. A thought that could never be soul to any activity would be more valuable to him than the perception of some vitality of relation demanding the activity of the whole being. He would call thoughts the stars that glorify the firmament of humanity, but the stars of his firmament were merely atmospheric—pretty fancies, external likenesses. That the grandest thing in the world is to be an accepted poet, is the despotic craze of a vast number of the weak-minded and half-made of both sexes. It feeds poetic fountains of plentiful yield, but insipid and enfeebling flow—the mere sweat of weakness under the stimulus of self-admiration.

Chapter 4.

THINKS AND THINGS

Walter was the very opposite of the Molly he counted common-place and outside the region of poetry, for she had a passion for turning a *think* into a *thing*. She had a strong instinctive feeling that she was in the world to do something, and she saw that if nobody tried to keep things right, they would go terribly wrong; what then could she be there for but to set or keep things right? And if she could do nothing with the big things, she must be the busier with the little things! Besides, who could tell how much the little might have to do with the big? The whole machine depended on every tiny wheel! She could not order the clouds, but she could keep some weeds from growing; and then when the rains came, they would not take away the good of it.

The world could be divided into people who let things go and those who do not; into the forces and facts as against the slaves and fancies; those who are always doing something along God's creative lines as opposed to those who are always grumbling and striving against them.

"Another penny for your thoughts, Walter!" said Molly.

"I am not going to deal with you. This time you would not think it worth a penny. Why are you so inquisitive about my thoughts?"

"I want to know what you meant when you said the other day that thoughts are better than things."

Walter hesitated. The question was an inclined plane leading to unknown depths of argument!

"See, Walter," said Molly, "here is a flower—a narcissus—a pheasant's eye; tell me the thought that is better than this thing!"

How troublesome girls were when they asked questions!

"Well," he said, not very logically, "that narcissus has nothing but air around it; my thought of the narcissus has mind around it."

"Then a thought is better than a thing because it has thought around it?"

"Well, yes."

"Did the thing come here of itself, or did it come of God's thinking?"

"Of God's thinking."

"And God is always the same?"

"Yes."

"Then God's thought surrounds the narcissus still, and so the narcissus is better than your thought of it!"

Walter was silent.

"I should so like to understand!" said Molly. "If you have a thought more beautiful than the narcissus, Walter, I should like to see it! Only, if I could see it, it would be a thing, would it not? A thing must be a think before it can be a thing. A thing is a ripe think, and must be better than a think—unless it loses something in ripening, which may very well be with man's thoughts, but hardly with God's! I will keep in front of the things, and look through them to the thoughts behind them. I want to understand! If a thing were not a thought first, it would not be worth anything! And every thing has to be thought about, else we don't see what it is! I haven't got it quite!"

Instead of replying, Walter rose, and they walked to the house side by side in silence.

"Could a thought be worth anything that God had never cared to think?" said Molly to herself as they went.

the hunt after new fancies. She watched for them, stalked them, followed them like a boy with a butterfly net. She caught them too, of the sort she wanted, plentifully. But none ever came to anything, so far as I could see. She never did anything with one of them. Whatever she caught had a cage to itself, where it sat on 'the all-alone stone.' Every other moment, while you and Mr. Dobson were talking, she would cry 'Oh! Oh! O—o—oh!' and pull out her notebook from the cork box in which she pinned her butterflies. She must have had a whole museum of ideas! The most accidental resemblance between words would suffice to start one; she would go after it, catch it, pin it down, and call it a correspondence. Now and then a very pretty notion would fall to her net, and often a silly one; but all were equally game to her.

"I found her amusing and interesting for days, but then began to see that she only led nothing nowhere. She was touchy and jealous, and said things that disgusted me; she never did anything for anybody; and though she hunted religious ideas most, she never seemed to imagine they could have anything to do with her life. It was only the fineness of a good thought that she seemed to prize. She would startle you any moment by an exclamation of delight at some religious fancy or sentimentality, and down it must go in her book, but it went no further. She was just as common as before, vulgar even, in her judgments of motives and actions. She seemed made for a refined and delicate woman, but would not take the trouble to be what she was made for. You told me, you know, that God makes us, but *we* have to be. She talked about afflictions as one might of manure—by these afflictions, of which she would complain bitterly, she was being fashioned for life eternal! It was all the most dreary, noisome rubbish I had ever come across. I used to lie awake thinking what could ever rouse such a woman to see that she had to *do* something—that neither man nor woman can become anything without having a hand in the matter. She seemed to expect the Spirit of God to work in her like yeast in flour, although there was not a sign of the dough rising. That is how I came to see that one may have any number of fine thoughts and fancies and be nothing the better, any more than the poor woman in the Gospel with her doctors! And when Walter, the next time he came home, talked as he did about thoughts and quoted Keats to the same effect, as if the finest thing in the universe were a fine thought, I could not bear it, and that made me speak to him as I did."

"You have made it very clear, Molly, and I quite agree with you. Thinks are of no use except they be turned into things."

"But perhaps, after all, I may have been unfair to her!" said Molly. "People are so peculiar! They seem sometimes to be altogether made up of odd bits of different people. There's Aunt Ann now! She would not do a tradesman out of a ha'penny, but she will cheat at backgammon!"

"I know she will, and that is why I never play with her, even though it is so seldom she will give herself any recreation that it makes me sorry to refuse her."

"There is one thing that troubles me," said Molly after a little pause.

"What is it, my child? I always like to hear that something troubles you, for then I know you are going to have an answer. To know that you are lacking a thing is the preparation for receiving it."

"I can't care—much—about poetry, and Walter says such fine things about it! Walter is no fool!"

"Far from one, I am glad to think!" said Richard, laughing. He found Molly's straightforward, humble confidence as delightful as amusing.

"It seems to me so silly to scoff at things because you can't go in for them!" she continued. "I sometimes hear people make insulting remarks about music, which I *know* to be a good and precious and lovely thing. Then I think with myself, they must be in the same condition with regard to music that I am with regard to poetry. So I take care not to be a fool in talking about what I don't know. That I am stupid is no reason for being a fool. Anyone whom God has made stupid has a right to be stupid, but no right to call others fools because they are not stupid."

"I thought you liked poetry, Molly!"

"So I do when *you* read it or talk about it. It seems as if you made your way of it grow to be my way of it. I hear the poetry and feel your feeling of it. But when I try to read it myself, then I don't care for it. Sometimes I turn it into prose, and then I get ahold of it."

"That is about the best and hardest test you could put it to, Molly! But perhaps you have been trying to like what does not deserve to be liked. There is much in the shape of poetry that would be worth nothing, even if it were set in gold and diamonds."

"I think the difficulty is in myself. Sometimes I am in the fit mood, and other times not. A single line will now and then set something churning, churning in me, so that I cannot understand myself. It will make me think of music and sunrise and the wind and the song of the lark, and all lovely things. But sometimes prose will serve me the same. And the next minute, perhaps, either of them will be boring me more than I can bear! I know it is my own fault, but—"

"Stop there, Molly! It may sometimes be your own fault, but certainly not always! You are particular, little one, and in exquisite things how can one be too particular? When Walter has gone to London, suppose we read a little more poetry together?"

Chapter 6.

A FATHER'S GIFT

Richard Colman had made some money in one of the good farming times, but of late had not been increasing his store. But he was a man too genuinely practical to set his mind upon money-making.

There are parents who, although they have found possession powerless for their own peace, nonetheless heap up for the sons coming after, in the weak but unquestioned fancy that possession will do for them what it could not do for their fathers and mothers. Richard was above such stupidity. He had early come to see that the best thing money could do for his son was to help prepare him for some work fit to employ what faculty had been given him, in accordance with the tastes also given him. He saw the last thing a foolish father will see—that the best a father can do is to enable his son to earn his livelihood in the exercise of a genial and righteous labor. He saw that possession generates artificial and enfeebling wants, overlaying and smothering the God-given necessities of our nature, whence alone issue golden hopes and manly endeavors.

He had therefore been in no haste to draw from his son a declaration of choice as to profession. When every man shall feel in himself a call to this or that, and scarce needs make a choice, the generations will be well served; but that was not yet, for what Walter was fit for was not yet quite manifest. It was only clear to the father that his son must labor for others with a labor, if possible, whose reflex action should be life to himself. Agriculture seemed inadequate to the full employment of the

27

gifts which, whether from paternal partiality or genuine insight, he believed his son to possess; neither had Walter shown inclination or aptitude for any department of it. All Richard could do, therefore, was to give him such preparation as would be a foundation for any pursuit; he might, he hoped, turn to medicine or the law.

Partly for financial reasons, he sent him to Edinburgh. There Walter neither distinguished nor disgraced himself, and developed no inclination to one more than another of the careers open to a young man of education. He read a good deal, however, and showed taste in literature—was, indeed, regarded by his companions as an authority in its more imaginative ranges, and especially in matters belonging to verse, having an exceptionally fine ear for its vocal delicacies. This is one of the rarest of gifts, but rarity does not determine value, and Walter greatly overestimated its relative importance. The consciousness of its presence had far more than a reasonable share in turning his thoughts to literature as a profession.

When Walter's bent became apparent, it troubled his father a little. He knew that to gain the level of excellence in that calling to ensure the merest livelihood required, in most cases, a severe struggle; and for such effort he doubted his son's capacity, perceiving in him none of the stoic strength that comes of a high ideal, and can encounter disappointment, even privation, without injury. Other and deeper dangers the good parent did not see. He comforted himself that even if things went no better than now, he could at least give his son a fair chance of discovering whether the career would suit him, and support him if it did suit him, until he should attain the material end of it.

Long before Miss Hancock's attack upon his supposed indifference to his son's idleness, he had made up his mind to let Walter try how far he could go in the way to which he was drawn. The next day he told his son, to his unspeakable delight, that he was ready to do what lay in his power to further his desire; that his own earthly life was precious to him only for the sake of the children he must by and by leave; and that when he saw him busy, contented, and useful, he would gladly yield his hold upon it.

Walter's imagination took fire at the prospect of realizing all

28

he had longed for but feared to subject to paternal scrutiny. He was at once eager to go out into the great unhomely world, in the hope of being soon regarded by his peers as the possessor of certain gifts and faculties which had not yet handed in their vouchers to himself. For, as the conscience of many a man seems never to trouble him until the looks of his neighbors bring their consciences to bear upon his, so the mind of many a man seems never to satisfy him that he has a gift until other men grant his possession of it. Around Walter, nevertheless, the world broke at once into rare bloom. He became like a windy day in the house, vexing his aunt with his loud foolish gladness, and causing the wise heart of Molly many a sudden, chilly foreboding. She knew him better than his father knew him. His father had not played with him day after day! She knew that happiness made him feel strong for anything, but that his happiness was easily dashed, and he was then a rain-wet, wind-beaten butterfly. He had no soul for bad weather, but he could not, therefore, be kept in wadding. He must have his trial; he must, in one way or another, encounter life, and disclose what amount of the real might be in him—what little but enlargeable claim he might have to manhood!

Chapter 7.

LONDON

Every morning, a man may say,
Calls him up with a new birthday;
Every day is a little life,
Sunny with love, stormy with strife:
Every night is a little death,
From which too soon he awakeneth ...

Walter wrote these lines, not knowing half what the words meant. As with the skirt of her mantle the dark wipes out the day, so with her sleep the night makes a man fresh for the new day's journey. If it were not for sleep, the world could not go on. To feel the mystery of day and night, to gaze into the far receding spaces of their marvel, is more than to know all the combinations of chemistry. A little wonder is worth tons of knowledge.

But to Walter the new day did not come as a call to new life in the world of will and action, but only as the harbinger of a bliss borne on the wind of the world. Was he not going forth to become a great man amongst great men? He would be strong among the weak! He would be great among the small! He did not suspect in himself what Molly saw or at least suspected in him. When a man is hopeful, he feels strong and can work. The thoughts come and the pen runs. Were he always at his best, what might not a man do! But not many can determine their moods; and none, be they poets or economists, can any more secure the conditions of ability than they can create ability.

When the mood changes and hope departs, the inward atmosphere is grown damp and dismal, there may be some whose imagination will yet respond to their call; but let some certain kind of illness come, and everyone must lose his power. His creature condition will assert itself, and he is compelled to discover that we did not create ourselves and do not live by ourselves.

Walter loved his father, but did not mind leaving him; he loved Molly, but did not mind leaving her; and we cannot blame him if he was glad to escape from his aunt. If people are not lovable, it takes a saint to love them, or at least one who is not afraid of them. Yet it was with a sense of somewhat dreary though welcome liberty that Walter found himself alone in London, but for the young man Harold Sullivan. With Sullivan's help he found a humble lodging not far from the British Museum, to the neighborhood of which his love of books led him.

For a time, feeling no necessity for immediate effort, he gave himself to the study of certain departments of our literature not previously within his easy reach. In the evening he would write or accompany his new friend to some lecture or amusement and so the weeks passed. To earn something seemed but a slowly approaching necessity, and the weeks grew to months. He was never idle, for his tastes were strong, and he had delight in his pen; but so sensitive was his social skin, partly from the licking of his aunt's dry, feline tongue, that he shrank from submitting anything he wrote even to Harold Sullivan who, a man of firmer and more world-capable stuff than he, would at least have shown him how things which the author saw and judged, from the inner side of the web, must appear on the other side. There are few weavers of thought capable of turning round the web and contemplating with unprejudiced regard the side of it about to be offered to the world, so as to perceive how it will look to eyes alien to its genesis.

Yet he did send poem after poem, now to this, now to that periodical, with the same result—that he never heard of them again. The verses, over which he labored with delight in the crimson glory they reflected on the heart whence they issued, were nothing in any eyes to which he submitted them. In truth, except for a good line here and there, they were by no means on the outer side what they looked to him on the inner. He read them in the light of the feeling in which he had written them; whoever else read them had not this light to interpret them by, had no correspondent mood ready to receive them. It was the business of the verse itself, by witchery of sound and magic of phrase, to arouse receptive mood, and of this it was incapable. A course of reading in the first attempts of such poets as rose after to well-merited distinction might reveal not a few things—among the rest, their frequent poverty.

Much mere babbling often issues before worthy speech begins. There was nothing in Walter's mind to be put in form except a few of the vague lovely sensations belonging to a poetic temperament. And as he read more and more, his inspiration came more and more from what he read, and less and less from knowledge of his own heart or the hearts of others. He had no revelation to give. He had, like most of our preachers, set out to run before he could walk, begun to cry aloud before he had any truth to utter—to teach, or at least to interest others, before he was himself interested in others. Now and then, especially when some fading joy of childhood gleamed up, words would come unbidden, and he would throw off a song destitute neither of feeling or music; but this kind of thing he scarcely valued, for it seemed to cost him nothing.

He comforted himself by concluding that his work was of a kind too original to be at once recognized by dulled and sated editors, and that he must labor on and keep sending.

"Why do you not write something?" Sullivan would ask, and Walter would answer, "My time has not yet come."

The friends he made were not many. Instinctively he shrank from what was coarse, feeling it destructive to every finer element. How could he write of beauty if, false to beauty, he had but for a moment turned to the unclean? But he was not satisfied with himself; while the recognition of the world was lacking, he felt he had done nothing.

He was in no anxiety, for he did not imagine it of consequence to his father whether he began a little sooner or a little later to earn. "The governor knows," he said to himself, "that to earn ought not to be a man's first object in life, even when necessity compels him to make it first in order of time—which is not the case with me!" But he did not ask himself whether he had substituted a better object. A greater man than himself, he reflected—no less a man, indeed, than Milton—had never earned a dinner till after he was thirty years of age! He did not consider how and to what ends Milton had all the time been diligent. He was no student yet of men's lives; he was interested almost only in their imaginations, and not fastidious enough as to whether those imaginations ran upon the rails of truth. He was rapidly filling his mind with the good and the bad of the literature of his country, but he had not yet gone far enough in distinguishing between the bad and the good in it. Books were to him the geological deposits of literary forces. He pursued his acquaintance with them to nourish the literary faculty in himself. They afforded him atmosphere and stimulant and store of matter. He was in full training for the profession that cultivates literature for and upon literature, and neither for nor upon truth.

Chapter 8.

THE RUIN OF DREAMS

A big stone fell suddenly into the smooth pool of Walter's conditions. A letter from his father brought the news that the bank where he had deposited his savings had proved but a swollen mushroom. He had lost all in the ruin.

"Indeed, my son," wrote the sorrowful Richard, "I do not see how with honesty to send you a shilling more! If you have exhausted the proceeds of my last check, and cannot earn a sufficiency, come home. Thank God, the land yet remains—so long as I can pay the rent."

A new impulse woke in Walter's heart, and he drew himself up for combat and endurance. He did not have much feeling for his father's trouble, but he would have scorned adding to it. He wrote at once that he must not think of him in the affair; he would do very well. It was not exactly a comforting letter, but it showed courage, and his father was glad.

Walter set himself to find employment in some mechanical department of literature—the only region in which he could think to do anything. When the architect comes to necessity, it is well if stones are near, and the mason's hammer; if he be not a better mason than he is an architect, alas for his architecture! Walter was nothing yet, however, neither architect nor mason, when the stern hand of necessity laid hold of him. But it is a fine thing for any man to be compelled to work. It is the first divine decree, issuing from love and knowledge. How would it have been with Adam and Eve had they been left to plenty and idleness, and the voice of God heard no more in the cool of the day?

But the search for work was a difficult and disheartening task. He who has encountered it, however, has had an experience whose value far more than equals its unpleasantness. A man out of work needs the God who cares for the sparrows, as much as does the man whose heart is torn with ingratitude, or crushed under a secret crime. Walter went hither and thither, communicated his quest to each of his few acquaintances, procured introductions, and even without any applied to some who might have employment to bestow, putting his pride into his pockets until they bulged. He walked till worn with weariness, giving good proof that he was no fool, but had the right stuff in him. He neither yielded to false fastidiousness nor relaxed his effort because of disappointment, not even when disappointment became the very atmosphere of his consciousness.

To the father it would have been the worst of his loss to see his son wiping the sweat and dust from the forehead his mother had been so motherly proud of, and to hear the heavy sigh with which he would sink into the not-too-easy chair that was all his haven after the tossing of the day's weary ground swell. He did not rise quite above self-pity, for he thought he was hardly dealt with; but so long as he did not respond to the foolish and weakening sentiment by relaxation of effort, it could not do him much harm; he would soon grow out of it, and learn to despise it. What one man has borne, why should not another bear? Why should it be unfit for him any more than the other? Certainly he who has never borne has yet to bear. The new experience is awaiting every member of the Dives clan. Walter wore out his shoes and could not buy another pair; his clothes grew shabby and he must wear them. It was no small part of his suffering, to have to show himself in a guise which made him so unlike the Walter he felt. But he did not let his father know even a small part of what he confronted.

He had never drawn close to his father and, therefore, they had come to no spiritual contact. Walter, the gentleman, saw only Richard, the farmer. He knew him as an honorable man, and in a way honored him; but he would have been dissatisfied with him in such society to which he considered himself belonging. It is a sore thing for a father, when he has shoved his son up a craggy steep, to see him walk away without looking behind.

Walter now had to give up his lodging. Sullivan took him into his own, doing all he could in return for his father's kindness.

Where now was Walter's poetry? Naturally, vanished. He was man enough to work, but not man enough to continue a poet. How could such a weary man stand the spur of the creative urge?

But to bestir himself was better than to make verses; and, indeed, of all the labors for a livelihood in which a man may cultivate verse, that of literature is the last he should choose. Compare the literary efforts of Burns with the songs he wrote when home from his plow!

Walter's hope had begun to faint outright, when Sullivan came in one evening. Sullivan told him that he had just met the editor of a new periodical, *The Field Battery,* who would make a place for Walter. The wages could suffice only for a grinding economy, but it was bread! More, it was work, and an opening to possibilities! Walter felt himself equal to any endurance short of incapacitating hunger, and gladly accepted the offer. His duty was the merest haphazard gathering of insignificant tasks, but even in that he might show ability, and who could tell what might follow. It was wearisome but not arduous, and above all, it would leave him time.

Chapter 9.

THE FIELD BATTERY

Walter found that compulsory employment, while taking from his time for genial labor, quickened his desire after it, increased his power for it, and made him more careful of his precious hours of leisure. Life now had an interest greater than before; and almost as soon as anxiety gave place, the impulse to utterance began again to urge him. Who can define this impulse or trace its origin? The result of it in Walter's case was ordered words, or poetry. Seldom is such a result of any value, but for the man, the process is invaluable. It remained to be seen whether it would benefit others as well as himself.

He became rapidly capable of better work. His duty was drudgery, but drudgery well encountered will reveal itself in a potent and precious refining, both intellectual and moral. One incapable of drudgery cannot be capable of the finest work. Many a man may do many things well, and be far from reception into the most ancient guild of workers.

Walter labored with conscience and diligence, and brought his good taste to tell on the quality of his drudgery. He is a contemptible workman who thinks of his claims before his duties, of his poor wages instead of his undertaken work. There was a strong sense of fairness in Walter; he saw the meanness of pocketing the poorest wages without giving good work in return. He saw that its own badness, and nothing else, makes any work mean—and the workman with it. That he believed himself capable of higher work was the worst of reasons for not giving money's worth for his money—that a thing is of little value is a poor excuse for giving bad measure of it. Walter carried his full load and was a man.

Sullivan was mainly employed in writing the reviews of "current literature." One evening he brought Walter a book of some pretension, told him he was hard-pressed, and begged him to write a notice of it. Walter, glad of the opportunity of both serving his friend and trying his own hand, set himself at once to read the book. The moment he thus took the attitude of a reviewer, he found the paragraph beginning, like potatoes, to sprout and generate other paragraphs. Between agreeing and disagreeing he had soon far more than enough to say, and sought his table as a workman seeks his bench.

To many people who think, writing is the greatest of bores; but Walter enjoyed it, even to the mechanical part of its operation. Heedless of the length of his article, he wrote until long after midnight, and next morning handed the result to his friend, who burst out laughing.

"Here's a paper for a quarterly!" Sullivan cried. "Man, it is almost as long as the book itself! This will never do! The world has neither time, space, money, or brains for so much! But I will take it, and see what can be done with it."

About a sixth part of it was printed, in which Walter could not recognize his hand; neither could he have gathered from it any idea of the book.

A few days after, Harold brought him a batch of books to review, taking care, however, to limit him to an average length for each. Walter entered thus upon a short apprenticeship—the end of which was that, a vacancy happening to occur, he was placed on the staff of the journal, to aid in reviewing the books sent by their publishers. His income was considerably augmented, but the work was harder and required more of his time.

From the first he was troubled to find how much more time and effort honesty demanded of him than pay made possible. He had not learned this while merely supplementing the labor of his friend, and taking his time. But now he became aware that to make acquaintance with a book, and pass upon it a justifiable judgment, required at least four times the attention he could afford it and still live. Many, however, he could knock off without compunction, regarding them as too slight to deserve attention. Indifferently honest, he was not so sensitive in justice as to reflect that the poorest thing has a right to fair play—that, free to say nothing, you must, if you speak, say the truth of the meanest. But Walter had not yet sunk to believe that there can be *necessity* for doing wrong. The world is divided, very unequally, into those who think a man cannot avoid doing wrong, and those who believe he *must* avoid doing wrong. The first live in fear of death; the latter set death in one eye and righteousness in the other.

Walter was compelled to print his first important review without having finished it. The next he worked at harder, and finished, but with less deliberation. He grew more and more careless toward the books he counted of little consequence, while he imagined himself growing more and more capable of getting at the heart of a book by skimming its pages. If skimming can ever be a true skill, it must come of long experience in the art of reading, and is not possible to a beginner. To skim and judge is to wake from a doze and give the charge to a jury.

Writing more and more smartly, he found the usual difficulty in abstaining from a smartness which was unjust because irrelevant. So far as his employers were concerned, Walter did his duty; but he forgot that apart from his obligation to the mere and paramount truth, it was from the books he reviewed— good, bad, or indifferent, whichever they were—that he drew the food he ate and the clothes that covered him.

His talent was increasingly recognized by the editors of the newspaper, and they began to put other—and what they counted more important work—his way, entrusting him with the discussion of certain social questions of the day. Like many another youth of small experience, he found it the easier to give a confident opinion that his experience was so small. In general he wrote logically and, which is rarer, was even capable of being made to see where his logic was wrong. But his premises were much too scanty, for what he took for granted was very often by no means granted. It mattered little to the editors or owners, however, so long as his writing was lucid, sparkling, and "crisp," leaving those who read willing to read more from the same pen.

Chapter 10.

FLATTERY

Within a year Walter began to be known—in the profession, at least—as a promising writer. To more than a few, he was already personally known as a very agreeable, gentlemanly fellow, so that in the following social season he had a good many invitations. It was by nothing beyond the ephemeral that he was known; but may not the man who has invented a good umbrella one day build a good palace?

His acquaintance was considerably varied, but of the social terraces above the professional, he knew nothing for a time.

One evening, however, he happened to be presented to Lady Tremaine. She had asked to have introduced to her the refined-looking young man, whom she had just heard was one of the principal writers for *The Field Battery*. She was a matronly, handsome woman, with cordial manners and a cold eye; frank, easy, confident, unassuming. Under the shield of her position, she would walk straight up to any subject and speak her mind of it plainly. It was more than easy to become acquainted with her when she chose.

The company was not a large one, and they soon found themselves alone in a quiet corner.

"They tell me you are a celebrated literary man, Mr. Colman," said Lady Tremaine.

"Not in the least," answered Walter. "I am but a poor hack."

"It is well to be modest, but I am not bound to take your description of yourself. Your class at least is in a fair way to take the lead!"

"In what, pray?"

"In politics, in society, in everything."

"Your ladyship cannot think it desirable."

"I do not pretend to desire it. I am not false to my own people. But the fact remains that you are coming to the front, and we are falling behind. And the sooner you get to the front, the better it will be for the world, and for us too."

"I cannot say I understand you."

"I will tell you why. There are now no fewer than three aristocracies. There is one of rank and one of brains. I belong to the one, you to the other. But there is a third."

"If you recognize the rich as an aristocracy, you must allow me to differ from you—very much!"

"Naturally, I quite agree with you. But what can your opinion and mind avail against the rising popular tide? All the old families are melting away, swallowed by the *nouveaux riches*. I should not mind, or at least I should feel it in me to submit with a good grace, if we were pushed from our stools by a new aristocracy of literature and science; but I do rebel against the social *regime* which is every day more strongly asserting itself. All the gradations are fast disappearing; the palisades of good manners, dignity, and respect are vanishing with the hedges; the country is positively inundated with slang and vulgarity—all from the ill breeding, presumption, and self-satisfaction of new people."

Walter felt tempted to ask whether it was not the fault of the existent aristocracy in receiving and flattering them; whether it could not protect society if it would; whether in truth the aristocracy did not love and even honor money as much as they; but he was silent.

As if she read his thought, Lady Tremaine resumed, "The plague of it is that younger sons must live! Money they must have, and there's the gate off the hinges! The best and, indeed, the only thing to help is that the two other aristocracies make common cause to keep the rich in their proper place."

It was not a very subtle flattery, but Walter was pleased. The lady saw she had so far gained her end, for she had an end in view, and so changed the subject.

"You go out of an evening, I see!" she said at length. "I am glad. Some authors will not."

"I do when I can. The evening, however, to one who—who—"

"—has an eye on posterity! Of course! It is gold and diamonds! How silly all our pursuits must appear in your eyes! But I hope you will make an exception in my favor!"

"I shall be most happy," responded Walter coridally.

"I will not ask you to come and be absorbed in a crowd—not the first time at least! Could you not manage to come and see me?"

"I am at your ladyship's service," replied Walter.

"Then come—let me see—the day after tomorrow, about five o'clock, at 17 Goodrich Square."

Walter could not but be flattered that Lady Tremaine was so evidently pleased with him. She called his profession an aristocracy too! Therefore she was not patronizing him, but receiving him on the same social level! We cannot blame him for the inexperience which allowed him to hold his head a little higher as he walked home.

Chapter 11.

BY ARRANGEMENT

There was little danger of Walter forgetting the appointment, and Lady Tremaine received him with cordiality. By and by she led the way toward literature, and after they had talked of several new books, she said, "We in this house are not altogether strange to your profession. My daughter Lufa is an authoress in her way. You, of course, have never heard of her, but it is twelve months since her volume of verse came out."

Surely Walter had, somewhere about the time, when helping his friend Sullivan, seen a small ornate volume of verses, with a strange name like that on the title page. He had written a notice of it, but could not remember what he had written.

"*Autumn Leaves* was exceedingly well received—for a first, of course! Lufa hardly thought so herself, but I asked her what she could expect, altogether unknown as she was. Tell me honestly, Mr. Colman, is there not quite as much jealousy in your profession as in any other?"

Walter allowed it was not immaculate in respect of envy and evil speaking.

"You have so much opportunity for revenge, you see!" said Lady Tremaine, "and such a coat of darkness for protection! With a few strokes of the pen, a man may ruin his rival!"

"Scarcely that!" returned Walter. "If a book be good, the worst of us cannot do it much harm; nor do I believe there are more than a few in the profession who would condescend to give a false opinion upon the work of a rival, though, doubtless, personal feeling may pervert the judgment."

"That, of course," returned the lady, "is but human! You cannot deny, however, that authors occasionally make furious assaults on each other!"

"Authors ought not to be reviewers," replied Walter. "I fancy most reviewers avoid the work of even an acquaintance, not to say a friend or enemy."

The door opened, and what seemed to Walter as lovely a face as could ever have dawned on the world peeped in, and would have withdrawn.

"Lufa," called Lady Tremaine, "you need not go away. Mr. Colman and I have no secrets. Come and be introduced to him."

She entered—a small, pale creature, below the middle height, with the daintiest figure, and childlike eyes of dark blue, very clear and, for the occasion, "worn wide." Her hair was brown on the side of black, divided in the middle and gathered behind in a great mass. Her dress was white, with a shimmer of red about it, and a blush-rose in the front. She greeted Walter in the simplest, friendliest way, holding out her hand very frankly. Her features were no smaller than for her size they ought to be, in themselves perfect, Walter thought, and in harmony with her whole being and carriage. Her manner was a gentle, unassuming assurance—almost as if they knew each other, but had not met for some time. Walter felt some ancient primeval bond between them—dim but indubitable.

The mother withdrew to her writing table, and began to write, now and then throwing in a word as they talked. Lady Lufa seemed pleased with her new acquaintance, while Walter was bewitched. Bewitchment I take to be the approach of the real to our ideal. Perhaps upon that, however, depends even the comforting or the restful. In the heart of everyone lies the necessity for homeliest communion with the perfectly lovely— we are made for it. Yet so far are we in ourselves from the ideal—which no man can come near until absolutely devoted to its quest—that we continually accept that as sufficient which in truth falls far short.

"I think, Mr. Colman, I have seen something of yours! You do put your name to what you write?" said Lady Lufa.

"Not always," replied Walter.

"I think the song may have been yours!"

44

Walter had, for the first time, just published a thing of his own—but that it should have arrested the eye of this lovely creature! He acknowledged that he had printed a trifle in *The Observatory*.

"I was *charmed* with it!" said the girl, the word itself charmingly drawled.

"The merest trifle!" remarked Walter. "It cost me nothing." He meant what he said, unwilling to be judged by such a slight thing.

"That is the beauty of it!" she answered. "Your song left your soul as the thrush's leaves his throat! Should we prize the thrush's more if we came upon him practicing it?"

Walter laughed. "But we are not meant to sing like the birds!"

"That you could write such a song without effort shows you to possess the bird-gift of spontaneity."

Walter was surprised at her talk, and willing to believe it profound. "The will and the deed in one may be the highest art!" he said. "I hardly know."

"May I write music to it?" asked Lady Lufa, with an upward glance, sweet smile, and gently apologetic look.

"I am delighted that you should think of doing so, for it is more than it deserves!" answered Walter. "My only condition is that you will let me hear it."

"That you have a right to. Besides, I'd dare not publish it without knowing you liked it."

"Thank you so much! To hear you sing it will let me know at once whether the song itself be genuine."

"No, no! I may fail in my part, and yours be all I take it to be. But I shall not fail. It holds me too fast for that!"

"Then I may hope for a summons?" said Walter, rising.

"Before long. One cannot order the mood, you know!"

Chapter 12.

THE ROUND OF THE WORLD

Surely birds, when they leave the nest, carry their hearts with them. However, not a few humans leave their hearts behind them—too often, alas, to be sent for afterward. The whole round of the world, with many a cloud rack on the ridge of it and many a mist on top of that, rises between them and the eyes and hearts which gave their very life that they might live. Some as they approach middle age, some only when they are old, wake up to understand that they have parents. To some the perception comes with their children; to others with the pang of seeing them walk away lighthearted out into the world, as they themselves turned their backs on their parents: their children had been all their own, and now the children had done with them!

Less or more, have we not all thus taken our journey into a far country? But many a man of sixty is more of a son to the father gone from the earth, than he was while under his roof. What a disintegrated mass the world would be, what a lump of half-baked brick, if death were indeed the end of affection! If there were no more chance of setting right what was so wrong in the loveliest relations! How gladly would many a son, who once thought it a weariness to serve his parents, minister now to their lightest need! And in the boundless eternity, is there no help?

Walter was not a prodigal, but a well-behaved youth. He was *only* proud and thought much of himself; was *only* pharisaical, not hypocritical; was *only* neglectful of those nearest him, always polite to those comparatively nothing to him! Compassionate and generous to necessity, he let his father and his sister-cousin starve for the only real food a man can give—himself. As to Him who thought his very thoughts into him, he neither heeded Him nor mocked Him by merest ceremony. There are those who refuse God the draught of water He desires, on the ground that their vessel is not fit for Him to drink from; Walter thought his vessel too good to fill with the water fit for God to drink.

He had the feeling, far from worded but certainly in him, that he was a superior man to his father. But it is a fundamental necessity of the kingdom of heaven, impossible as it must seem to all outside it, that each shall count others better than himself. It is to be the natural condition of the man God made, in relation to the other men God has made. Man is made not to contemplate himself but to behold in others the beauty of the Father. A man who lives to meditate upon and worship himself is already in the slime of hell. Walter knew his father to be a well-read man, but because he had not been to a university, he placed no value on his reading. Yet this father was a man who had communion with high countries, communion in which his son would not have perceived the presence of an idea.

Therefore, Richard's mind, and the expression of his mind in his attitudes and behavior, must have been eminently acceptable to the ushers of those high countries; his was a certain quiet, simple, direct way, reminding one of Nathanael, in whom was no guile. In another man Walter would have called it *bucolic;* in his father he shut his eyes to it as well as he could, and was ashamed of it. In Walter's circle, Richard would scarcely be regarded as gentleman—he would look odd! Walter, therefore, had not encouraged the idea of Richard coming to see him. He was not satisfied with the father by whom the Father of fathers had sent him into the world! But Richard was the truest of gentleman. He was not only courteous and humble, but that rare thing—natural; and the natural, be it old as the Greek, must be beautiful. The natural dwells deep, and is not the careless, any more than are the studied or assumed.

Walter loved his father, but the root of his love did not go deep enough to send aloft a fine flower; to grow deep in is to branch high out. He seldom wrote, and then only briefly. He did not make a confidant of his father. He did not even tell him what he was doing, or what he hoped to do. He might mention a success; but of hopes, fears, aspirations, defeats, thoughts, or desires, he said nothing. As to his theories, he never imagined his father entering into such things as occupied his mind! The ordinary young man takes it for granted that he and the world are far ahead of "the governor;" the father may have left behind him, as nebulae sinking below the horizon of youth, those questions the younger world is but just waking up to.

The blame, however, may lie in part at the parent's door. The hearts of the fathers need turning to the children, as much as the hearts of the children need turning to the fathers. Few men open up to their children; and where a man does not, the separation begins with him, for all that his love may be deep and true. That it is unmanly to show one's feelings is a superstition prevalent with all English-speaking people. Now, wherever feeling means weakness, falsehood, or anxiety, it ought not to be shown, for it ought not even to exist! But for a man to hide from his son his loving and his loathing is to refuse him the divinest fashion of teaching. Richard read the best things, and loved the best writers; yet never once had he read a poem with his son, or talked to him about any poet! If Walter had even suspected his father's insight into certain things, he would have loved him more. As closely bound as they were, neither knew the other, and each would have been astonished at what he might have found in the other. The father might have discovered many handles by which to lay hold of his son; the son might have seen the same lamp bright in his father's chamber which he was himself now trimming in his own.

Chapter 13.

THE SONG

At length Lady Lufa summoned Walter to hear her music atop his verses. His poem was not much of a song, nor did he think it was.

> Mist and vapor and cloud
> Filled the earth and the air!
> My heart was wrapped in a shroud,
> And death was everywhere.
>
> The sun went silently down
> To his rest in the unseen wave;
> But my heart, in its purple and crown,
> Lay already in its grave.
>
> For a cloud had darkened the brow
> Of the lady who is my queen;
> I had been a monarch, but now
> All things had only been!
>
> I sprang from the couch of death:
> Who called my soul? Who spake?
> No sound! No answer! No breath!
> Yet my soul was wide awake!
>
> And my heart began to blunder
> Into rhythmic pulse the while;

I turned—away was the wonder—
My queen had begun to smile.

Out broke the sun in the west!
Out laughed the created sea!
And my heart was alive in my breast
With light, and love, and thee!

There was a little music in the verses, and they had a meaning, though not a very new or valuable one.

He went in the morning and was shown into the drawing room, his heart beating with expectation. Lady Lufa was alone and already at the piano. She wore a gray dress with red rosebuds, and looked as simple as any country parson's daughter. She gave him no greeting beyond a little nod, at once struck a chord or two, and then began to sing.

Walter was charmed. The singing, and the song through the singing, altogether exceeded his expectation. He had feared he should not be able to praise heartily, for he had not lost his desire to be truthful. But she was an artist! There was indeed nothing original in her music; it was mainly a reconstruction of common phrases afloat in the musical atmosphere. Yet she managed the slight dramatic element in the lyric with taste and skill, following the tone and sentiment with chord and inflection. Thus the music was worthy of the verses—which is not saying very much for either—while the expression the girl threw into the song went to the heart of the youth and made him foolish.

She ceased; he was silent for a moment, then fervent in thanks and admiration. "The verses are mine no more. I shall care for them now!"

"You won't mind if I publish them with the music?"

"I shall feel more honored than I dare tell you. But how am I to go to my work after this taste of paradise? It was too cruel of you, Lady Lufa, to make me come in the morning."

"I am very sorry!"

"Will you grant me one favor to make up?"

"Yes."

"Never sing the song to anyone when I am present. I could not bear it."

50

"I promise," she answered, looking up into his face with a glance of sympathetic consciousness.

There was an acknowledged secret between them, and Walter hugged it.

"I gave you a frozen bird," he said, "and you have warmed it and made it soar and sing."

"Thank you! A very pretty compliment!" she answered, and there was a moment's silence. "I am so glad we know each other!" she resumed. "You could help me so much if you would! Next time you come, you must tell me something about those old French rhymes that have come into fashion of late! They say a pretty thing so much more prettily for their quaint, antique, courtly liberty! The triolet now—how deliciously impertinent it is, is it not?"

Walter knew nothing about the old French modes of verse. Unwilling to place himself at a disadvantage, he made an evasive reply and went. But when at length he reached home, it was with several ancient volumes in his pockets and hands. Before an hour was over, he was wrapped in delight with the variety of dainty modes in which, by shape and sound, a very pretty French something was carved out of nothing at all. Their fantastic surprises, the ring of their bell-like returns upon themselves, their music of triangle and cymbal, gave him quite a new pleasure. In some of them poetry seemed to approach the nearest possible to birdsong, imitating the careless, impromptu warblings as old as the existence of birds, and as new as every fresh individual joy. Each new generation grows its own feathers and sings its own song, yet always the feathers and the song of its own kind.

The same night he sent her the following triolet.

> Oh, why is the moon
> Awake when thou sleepest
> To the nightingale's tune?
> Why is the moon
> Making a noon
> When night is the deepest?
> Why is the moon
> Awake when thou sleepest?

In the evening there came a little note to him, with a coronet on the paper, but neither date nor signature. "Perfectly delicious! How *can* such a little gem hold so much color? Thank you a thousand times!"

Chapter 14.

THE FACE OF LUFA

By this time Walter was in love with Lady Lufa. He said as much to himself, at least, and in truth he was almost possessed with her. Every thought that rose in his mind began at once to drift toward her. Every hour of the day had a rosy tinge from the dress in which he first saw her.

One might write a long essay on this general phenomenon called *love,* and yet contribute little to the understanding of it in the individual case. Its kind is to be interpreted after the kind of person who loves. There are as many hues and shades and forms and constructions of love as there are human countenances, hearts, judgments, and schemes of life. Walter had not been an impressionable youth, because he had an imagination which both made him fastidious and stood him in stead of falling in love. When a man can give form to things that move him, he is less driven to fall in love. But now Walter saw everything through a window, and the window was the face of Lufa. His thinking was always done in the presence and light of that window. She seemed an intrinsic component of each of his mental operations. In every beauty and attraction of life he saw her. He was possessed by her, almost as some are possessed by evil spirits. And to be possessed, even by a human being, may be to take refuge in the tombs, there to cry and cut one's self with fierce thoughts.

But Walter was not yet troubled. He lived in love's eternal presence and did not look forward. Even jealousy had not yet begun to show itself in any shape. He was not in Lady Lufa's

53

social set, and therefore not much drawn to conjecture what might be going on. In the glamour of literary ambition, he took for granted that Lady Lufa allotted his world a higher orbit than that of her social life, and prized most the pleasures they had in common, which so few were capable of sharing.

She had indeed in her own circle never found one who knew more of the refinements of verse than a schoolgirl does of Beethoven; and it was a great satisfaction to her to know one who not merely recognized her proficiency, but could guide her further into the depths of an art which everyone thinks he understands, and only one here and there does. Therefore, she was able to give him a real welcome when they met, as they did again and again during the season. How much she cared for him, my reader shall judge. I think she cared for him very nearly as much as for a dress made to her liking. An injustice from him would have brought the tears into her eyes. A poem he disapproved of she would have thrown aside, perhaps into the fire.

She did not, however, submit much of her work to Walter's judgment. She was afraid that his opinion might put her out of heart with it. Before making his acquaintance, she had a fresh volume, a more ambitious one, well on its way to completion, but fearing lack of his praise, had said nothing to him about it. And besides this diffidence, she did not wish to appear to solicit from him a good review. She might cast herself on his mercy, but it should not be confessedly. She had pride, though not conscience, in the matter. The mother was capable of begging, not the daughter. She might use fascination, but never en- treaty—that would be to degrade herself!

Walter had, of course, taken a second look at her first vol- ume. What he had said of it in his review was true; but now he saw that, had he been anxious to praise, he might have found passages to commend, or in which, at least, he could have pointed out merit. But no allusion was made to the book, on the one hand because Lady Lufa was aware he had written the review, and on the other because Walter did not wish to give his opinion of it. He placed it in the category of first works; and, knowing how poor those of afterwards distinguished writers may be, it did not annoy him that one who could talk so well should have written such rubbish.

Lady Lufa had indeed a craze for composition, and the indul-
gence of it was encouraged by her talent. However, there was
no reason in heaven, earth, or the other place, why what she
wrote should see the light, for it had little to do with light of
any sort. *Autumn Leaves* had had no such reception as her mother would have Walter believe. Lady Tremaine was one of those
"good mothers" who, like "good churchmen," will wrong any
other to fulfill desires of their own. She had paid her court to
Walter that she might gain a reviewer who would yield her
daughter what she called justice; for the sake of justice she
would curry favor! A half-merry, half-retaliative humor in Lufa
may have sought for revenge by making Walter fall in love with
her. At all events, it consoled her wounded vanity when she saw
him in love with her; but it was chiefly in the hope of a good
review of her next book that she had cultivated his acquaintance, and now she felt sure of her end.

Most people liked Walter, even when they laughed at his
simplicity, for it was the simplicity of a generous nature; we
cannot, therefore, wonder if he was too confident, and from
Lady Lufa's behavior presumed to think she looked upon him
as worthy of a growing privilege. If she regarded literature as
she professed to regard it, he had but to distinguish himself, he
thought, to be more acceptable than wealth or nobility could
have made him. As to material possibilities, the youth never
thought of them; a worshiper does not meditate on how to feed
his goddess! Lady Lufa was his universe and everything in it—a
small universe and scantily furnished for a human soul, had she
been the prime of women! He scarcely thought of his home
now, or of the father who had made it home. As to God, it is a
question whether he had ever thought of Him. For can that be
called thinking of another, which is the mere passing of a name
through the mind, without one following thought of relation or
duty? Many think it a horrible thing to say there is no God, who
never think how much worse a thing it is not to heed Him. If
God be not worth minding, what great ruin can it be to imagine
His nonexistence?

What, then, had Walter made of it by leaving home? He had
almost forgotten his father; he had learned to be at home in
London; he had passed many judgments, some of them more
or less unjust; he had printed enough for a volume of little

better than truisms concerning life, society, fashion, dress, etc; he had published two or three rather nice songs, and had a volume of poems almost ready; he had kept himself the greater part of the time, and had fallen in love with an earl's daughter.

Upon one of his visits, the same earl's daughter said to him, "Everybody has gone back to the country, and so shall we—tomorrow."

"Today," he rejoined, "London is full; tomorrow it will be a desert!"

She looked up at him, and did not seem glad.

"I have enjoyed the season so much!" she said. He thought her lip trembled. "But you will come and see us at Comberidge, will you not?" she added.

"Do you think your mother will ask me?" he said.

"I think she will. I do so want to show you our library! And I have so many things to ask you!"

"I am your slave, the genie of your lamp."

"I would I had such a lamp as would call you!"

"It will need no lamp to make me come."

Lamps to call moths are plenty, and Lufa was herself one.

vailing delirious fancies. He remembered his mother's last rebuke—for insolence to a servant; remembered her last embrace, her last words; and his heart turned tenderly to his father. Yet when he entered the house and faced the old surroundings, an unexpected gloom overclouded him. Had he been heart-free and humble, they would have been full of delight for him; but pride had been busy in his soul, and its home was in higher planes! How many essential refinements, as he foolishly and vulgarly counted them, were lacking here! What would Lady Lufa think of his surroundings? Did it well become one of the second aristocracy? His world had gradually been filling him with a sense of importance which had no being except in his own brain, and the notion took the meanest of mean forms—that of looking down on his own history. He was still too much of a gentleman not to repress the show of the feeling, but its mere presence caused a sense of alienation between him and his. When the first greetings were over, nothing came readily to follow. The wave had broken on the shore, and there was not another behind it. Things did not, however, go badly; for the father when disappointed always tried to account for everything to the advantage of the other; and on his part, Walter did his best to respond to his father's loving courtesy. He was not of such as keep no rule over themselves; not willingly would he allow discomfort to wake temper; he did not brood over defect in those he loved; but it did comfort him that he was so soon to leave his uncongenial surroundings, and go where all would be as gentleman desired to see it.

No one needs to find it hard to believe such snobbishness could exist in a youth gifted like Walter Colman; for a sweet temper, fine sympathies, and warmth of affection cannot be called a man's own, so long as he has felt and acted without cooperation of the will. Walter had never yet fought a battle within himself, had never set his will against his inclination. He had, indeed, bravely fronted the necessity of the world, but we cannot regard it as *assurance* of a noble nature that one is ready to labor for the things that are needful. A man is indeed contemptible who is not ready to work; but not to be contemptible is hardly to be honorable. Walter had never actively chosen the right way or put out any energy to walk in it. There are usurers and sinners nearer the kingdom of heaven than many a respectable, socially successful youth of education and ambition. Walter was not simple. He judged things not in themselves, but after an artificial and altogether foolish standard, for his aim was a false one—social distinction.

The ways of his father's house were nowise sordid, though so simple that his losses had made scarcely a difference in them; they were hardly even humble—only old-fashioned—but Walter was ashamed of them. He even thought it unladylike of Molly to rise from the table to wait on her uncle or himself; and once, when she brought the teakettle in her own little hand, he actually reproved her.

The degrading influences of modern times have given us the notion that success lies in reaching the modes of life in the next higher social stratum; the fancy that those ways are standard of what is worthy, becoming, or proper; and the idea that our standing is determined by our knowledge of what is or is not *the thing*. It is only the lack of dignity and courtesy that makes such points of any interest or consequence.

Fortunately for Walter's temper, his aunt was discreetly silent, too busy taking the youth's measure afresh to talk much, too intent on material wherewith to make up her mind concerning him. She had had to alter her idea of him as incapable of providing his own bread and cheese; but what reflection of him was henceforth to inhabit the glass of her judgment, she had not yet determined, except that it should be unfavorable.

It was a relief when bedtime came, and he was alone in what was always called his room. He soon fell asleep, to dream of Lufa and the luxuries about her—luxuries which had accumulated to the point of encumbrance, and so were now even opposed to comfort. How different his thoughts from those of the father who kneeled in the moonlight at the side of his own bed, and said something to Him who never sleeps! When Walter woke, his first feeling was a pang, for the things about him were as walls between him and Lufa.

He avoided any tête-à-tête with Molly. He had no true idea of the girl, and was not capable of one. She was a whole nature; he was of many parts, not yet begun to cohere. This unlikeness, probably, was at the root of his avoidance of her. Perhaps he had an undefined sense of rebuke, and feared her without being aware of it. Never going further than halfway into a thing, he had never relished Molly's questions. They went deep into issues where he saw no difficulty, and he was not even conscious of the darkness upon which Molly desired light cast. And now when he became aware that Molly was looking at him, he did not like it; he felt as if she saw some lack of harmony between his consciousness and his history. He was annoyed, even irritated, with the olive-cheeked, black-eyed girl, who for so many years had been like his sister; she was making remarks upon him in that questioning laboratory of her brain!

Molly was indeed trying to understand what had caused this difference between them. She had never felt Walter come very near her, for he was not one who had learned, or would easily learn, to give himself; and the man who does not give at least something of himself, gives nothing; but now she knew that he had gone further away, and she saw his father look disappointed. To Molly it was a sad relief when his departure came. They had not once disputed, but she had not once offered him a penny for his thoughts, or asked him a single question. He did not want her to go to the station with him.

Chapter 16.

A MIDNIGHT REVIEW

From Comberidge a dogcart had been sent to meet Walter at the railway. He drove up the avenue as the sun was setting behind the house, and its long, low, terraced front received him into cold shadow. The servant who opened the door said her ladyship was on the lawn; following him across the hall, Walter came out into the glory of a red sunset. Like a lovely carpet, or rather, like a silent river, the lawn appeared to flow from the house as from its fountain, issuing by the open doors and windows, and descending like a gentle rapid to lose itself far away among trees and shrubs. Over it were scattered groups and couples and individuals, looking like the creatures of a half-angelic paradise.

A little way off, under the boughs of a huge beech tree, Lufa sat reading, with a pencil in her hand as if she made notes. As he stepped from the house, she looked up and saw him. She laid her book on the grass, rose and came toward him. He went to meet her, but the light of the low sun was directly in his eyes, and he could not see her shadowed face. When her voice of welcome came in the luminous darkness, their hands found each other. He thought hers trembled, but it was his own. She led him to her mother.

"I am glad to see you," said Lady Tremaine. "You are just in time!"

"For what, may I ask?" returned Walter.

"It is out at last!"

"No, mamma," interrupted Lufa. "The book is not out! It is

almost ready, but I have only had one or two early copies. I am so glad Mr. Colman will be the first to see it! He will prepare me for the operation!"

"What do you mean?" asked Walter, bewildered. It was the first time he had heard of her new book.

"Of course I shall be cut up! The weekly papers especially would lose half their readers if they did not go in for vivisection! But mamma shouldn't have asked you now!"

"Why?"

"Well, you mightn't—I shouldn't like you to feel an atom less comfortable in speaking your mind."

"There is no fear of that sort in my thoughts," answered Walter, laughing. But it troubled him a little that she had not let him know what she was doing. "Besides," he went on, "you need never know what I think. There are other reviewers on the *Battery!*"

"I should recognize your hand anywhere! And more than that, I should only have to pick out the most rigid and unbending criticism to know which must be yours. It is your way, and you know it! Are you not always showing me up to myself? That's why I was in such mortal terror of your finding out what I was doing. If you had said anything to make me hate my work," she went on, looking up at him with earnest eyes, "I should never have touched it again; and I did want to finish it! You have been my master now for—let me see—how many months? I do not know how I shall ever thank you!" Here she changed her tone. "If I come off with a pound of flesh left, it will be owing entirely to the pains you have taken with me! I wonder whether you will like any of my triolets! But it is time to dress for dinner, so I will leave you in peace—but not all night, for when you go to bed you shall take *your* copy with you to help you fall asleep."

While dressing, he was full of the dread of not liking the book well enough to praise it as he wished. A first book was nothing, he said to himself; it might be what it would, but the second—that was another matter! He recalled what first books he knew. "Poems by Two Brothers" gave not a foretaste of what was to come so soon after them! Shelley's prose attempts in his boyhood were below criticism! Byron's "Hours of Idleness" were as idle as he called them! He knew what followed these and others, but what had followed Lady Lufa's? What if it should be no better than what preceded? For his own part he did not, he would not, much care. It was not for her poetry, it was for herself he loved her! What she wrote was not she, and could make no difference. It was not as if she had no genuine understanding of poetry, no admiration or feeling for it. A poet could do well enough with a wife who never wrote a verse, but hardly with one who had no natural relation to it, no perception of it! A poet in love with one who laughed at his poetry! What or wherein could be their relation to each other?

He is a poor poet—and Walter was such a poet—who does not know there are better things than poetry. Keats began to discover it just before he died.

Walter feared therefore the coming gift, as he might that of a doubted enchantress. It was nonetheless a delight, however, to remember that she said, "Your copy." But he must leave thinking and put on his necktie! There are other things than time and tide that wait for no man!

Going in to dinner, Lady Tremaine gave him Lufa, who took his arm with old familiarity. The talk at table was what it could hardly help being—only for Walter it was talk with Lufa! The pleasure of talk often owes not much to the sense of it. There is more than the intellect concerned in talk; there is more at its root than fact or logic or lying.

When the scene changed to the drawing room, Lufa played tolerably and sang well, delighting Walter. She asked and received his permission to sing "my song," as she called it, and pleased him with it more than ever. He managed to get her into the conservatory, which was large, and there he talked much, and she seemed to listen much. It was but the vague, twilit, allusive talk which, coming readily to all men in love, came the more readily to one always a poet, and not merely a poet by being in love. Every one in love sees a little further into things, but few see clearly, and hence love-talk has in general so little meaning. Ordinary men in love gain glimpses of truth other than they usually see, but from having so little dealing with the truth, they do not even try to grasp it; they do not know it for truth even when dallying with it. It is the true man's dreams that come true.

He raised her hand to his lips as at length she turned toward the drawing room, and he thought she more than yielded it, but could not be sure. Anyhow she was not offended, for she smiled her usual sweetness as she bade him good-night.

"One instant, Mr. Colman!" she added. "I promised you a sedative! I will run and get it. No, I won't keep you—I will send it to your room."

He had scarce shut his own door upstairs when it opened again, and there was Lufa.

"I beg your pardon!" she said. "I thought you would not be up here yet, and I wanted to make my little offering with my own hand; it owes so much to you!"

She slipped past him, laid her book on his table, and went.

He lighted his candles with eager anxiety, and took up the book. It was a dramatic poem of some length, daintily bound in white vellum, with gilt edges. On the title page was written "the Master's copy," with the date and Lufa's initials. He threw himself into a great soft chair that invited him with open arms, and began to read.

He had taken champagne pretty freely at dinner; his mind was yet in the commotion left by the summer wind of their many words that might mean so much; and he felt his kiss of her dainty hand, and her pressure of it to his lips. As he read, she seemed still and always in the doorway, entering with the book; and its inscription was continually turning up with a shine—such was the mood in which he read through the poem, every word, some of them many times; then he rose and went to his writing table, to set down his judgment of his lady's poem. He wrote and wrote, almost without pause. Then dawn began to glimmer, and the red blood of the morning came back to chase the swoon of the night before at last, throwing down his pen, he gave a sigh of weary joy, tore off his clothes, plunged into his bed, and there lay afloat on the soft waves of sleep. And as he slept, the sun came slowly up to shake the falsehood out of the earth.

Chapter 17.

A PALE REFLECTION

Walter slept until nearly noon, then rose, very weary but with a gladness at his heart. On his table were spread such pages as must please Lufa! His thoughts went back to the poem, but, to his uneasy surprise, he found he did not recall it with any special pleasure. He had felt great delight in reading it, and in giving shape to his delight, but he could not now think what it was that had given him such satisfaction. He had worked too long, he said to himself, and this was the reaction; he was too tired to enjoy the memory of what he had so heartily admired. Aesthetic judgment was so dependent on mood! He decided to glance over what he had done, correct it a little, and post it that afternoon, that it might appear in the next issue.

He drank the cup of cold tea by his bedside, sat down, and took up his hurriedly written sheets. He found in them much that seemed good work of his own; and the passages quoted gave ostensible ground for the remarks made upon them; but somehow the whole affair seemed quite different. The review would incline any lover of verse to read the book; and the passages cited were preceded and followed by rich and praiseful epithets; but neither quotations nor remarks moved in him any echo of response. He gave the manuscript what correction it required, laid it aside, and took up the poem.

What could be the matter? There was nothing but embers where had been glow and flame! Something must be amiss with him! He recalled an occasion on which, feeling similarly with regard to certain poems till then favorites, he was sorely troubled, but a serious attack of illness very soon relieved his perplexity. Something like it must surely be at hand to account for the contradiction between Walter last night and Walter this morning! Closer and closer he scanned what he read, peering if he might to its very roots, in agonized endeavor to see what he had seen as he wrote. But his critical consciousness neither acknowledged what he had felt, nor would grant him anything in a condition of poetic collapse.

He read on and on, read the poem through, turned back and read passage after passage again, but without one individual approach to the revival of former impression. "Commonplace! Commonplace!" echoed in his inner ear, as if whispered by some mocking spirit. He argued that he had often found himself too fastidious. His demand for finish ruined many of his verses, rubbing and melting and wearing them away, like frost and wind and rain, till they were worthless! The predominance and overkeenness of the critical had turned in him to disease! His eye was sharpened to see the point of a needle, but a tree only as a blotted mass! A man's mind was meant to receive as a mirror, not to concentrate rays like a convex lens! Was it not then likely that the first reading gave the true impression of the ethereal, the vital, the flowing, the iridescent? Did not the solitary and silent night brood like a hen on the nest of the poet's imaginings? Was it not the night that waked the soul? How then could the garish light of day afford the mood fit for judging a poem—the cold sick morning, when life is but half worth living!

Walter did not think how much champagne he had taken or how much that might have to do with one judgment at night and another in the morning. "Set one mood against another," he said, conscious all the time it was a piece of special pleading, "and one weighs as much as the other!" For it was horrible to him to think that the morning was clear-eyed, and that the praise he had lavished on the book was but a vapor of the night. How was he to carry himself to the lady of his love, who at most did not care half as much for him as for her book?

How poetry could be such a passion with her, when her own was but mediocre, was a question Walter dared not shape; not, however, that he saw the same question might be put with regard to himself, for his own poetry was neither strong nor fresh nor revealing. He had not noted that an unpoetic person will occasionally go into mild ecstasy over phrase or passage or verse in which a poet may see little or nothing.

He came back to this—one hour has as good a claim to insight as his other. If he saw the thing so once, why not say what he had seen? Why should the thing not stand? His consciousness of the night before had certainly been nearer that of a complete, capable being than that of today! He was in a higher human condition then than now!

But here came another doubt—what was he to conclude concerning other numerous judgments he had passed irrevocably? Was he called and appointed to influence the world's opinion of the labor of hundreds according to the mood he happened to be in, or the hour at which he read their volumes? But if he must write another judgment of that poem in vellum and gold, he must first pack his portmanteau! To write in her home as he felt now would be treachery.

Not confessing it, he was persuading himself to send on the review. Of course, had he the writing of it now, he would not write a paper like that! But the thing being written, it could claim as good a chance of being right as another. Had it not been written as honestly as another of today would be? Might it not be just as true? The laws of art are so undefined!

Thus on and on went the windmill of heart and brain, until at last the devil, or the devil's shadow—that is, the bad part of the man himself—got the better, and Walter, not being true, committed a lie and published the thing he would no longer have said. He thought he worshiped the truth, but he did not. He knew that the truth was everything, but a lie came that seemed better than the truth. In his soul he knew he was not acting truly; had he honestly loved the truth, he would not have played hocus-pocus with metaphysics and logic, but would have made haste to a manly conclusion. He took the packet, and on his way to the dining room, dropped it into the postbox in the hall.

During lunch he was rather silent and abstracted; the packet was not gone, and his conscience might yet commend him to recall it! When the appointed hour was past and the paper carried beyond his recovery, he felt easier, saying to himself that what was done could not be undone; he would be more careful another time. He was comforted that he had done no injustice to Lufa! He did not reflect that he had done her the greatest injustice in helping her to believe that worthy which was not worthy, herself worshipful who was not worshipful. He told her that he had finished her drama before going to bed, and was perfectly charmed with it. That it had as much exceeded his expectations then as it had fallen below them since, he did not say.

In the evening he was not so bright as before. Lufa saw it and was troubled. She feared he doubted the success of her poem. She led the way, and found he avoided talking about it. She feared he was not so well pleased with it as he had said. Walter asked if he might not read from it in the drawing room. She would not consent.

"None there are of our sort!" she said. "They think literature foolishness. Even my mother, the best of mothers, doesn't care about poetry, and cannot tell one measure from another. Come and read a page or two of it in the summerhouse in the wilderness instead. I want to know how it will sound in people's ears."

Walter was ready enough. He was fond of reading aloud, and believed he could so read the poem that he need not say anything. And certainly, if justice meant making the words express more than was in them, he did it justice. But in truth the situation was sometimes touching; and the more so to Walter that the hero of the poem was the lady's inferior in birth, means, and position—much more her inferior than Walter was Lufa's. The lady alone was on the side of the lowly born; father, mother, brothers, sisters, uncles, aunts, and cousins to the remotest degree stood against him even to hatred. The general pathos of the idea disabled the criticism of the audience, composed of the authoress and the reader, blinding perhaps both to not a little that was neither brilliant nor poetic. The lady wept at the sound of her own verses from the lips of one who was to her in the position of the hero toward the heroine; and the lover, critic as he was, could not but be touched when he saw her weep at passages suggesting his relation to her.

Therefore, when they found the hand of the one resting in that of the other, it did not seem strange to either. When suddenly the lady snatched hers away, it was only because a mischievous little bird, spying on them, and hurrying away to tell, made a great fluttering in the foliage. Then was Walter's conscience not a little consoled, for he was aware of a hearty love for her poem. Under such conditions he could have gone on reading it all the night!

Chapter 18.

A RIDE TOGETHER

Days passed, and things went on much the same. Walter dared not tell Lufa all he felt, but seized every opportunity of a tête-à-tête, and missed none of the proximity she allowed him. She never seemed other than pleased to be his companion; her ways with him were always pretty, and sometimes playful. She was almost studious to please him; and if she never took a liberty with him, she never resented any he took with her, which certainly were neither numerous nor daring, for Walter was not presumptuous, least of all with women.

But Lufa was careful not to neglect their other guests. She was always ready to accompany any of the ladies riding out of a morning; and a Mr. George Sefton, who was there with his sister when Walter arrived, generally rode with them. He was some distant cousin of Lufa and older than Walter. He had taken little notice of Walter, which Walter resented more than he would have cared to acknowledge. Sefton was tall and lanky, with a look of not having been in the oven quite long enough, but handsome nevertheless. Without an atom of contempt, he cared nothing for what people might think; and when accused of anything, he laughed and never defended himself. Having no doubt he was in the right, he had no anxiety as to the impression he might make. In the hunting field he was now reckless, now so cautious that the men would chaff him. But they knew well enough that whatever he did came either of pure whim or downright good sense; no one ever questioned his pluck.

It had been taken for granted by Lufa that Walter could not ride; whereas, not only had he some experience, but he was one of the few possessed of an individual influence over the lower brotherhood of animals, and especially the equine.

One morning, as one of the horses was ailing, Lufa found that the choice of her mount required consideration. Sefton said the horse he had been riding would carry her perfectly.

"What will you do for a horse?" she asked.

"Go without."

"What shall we do for a gentleman?"

"Go without."

"I saw the groom this morning," suggested Walter, "on a lovely little roan!"

"Ah, Red Racket!" answered Lady Lufa. "He is no horse—he is a little fiend. Goes as gently as a lamb with my father, though, or anyone that he knows can ride him. Try Red Racket, George."

"I would if I could sit him. But I'm not a rough rider, and much disinclined to have my bones broken. It's not as if there was anything to be gained by it!"

"Two hours of your sister, your cousin, and their friend!"

"Much of you I should have with Red Racket under me—or as likely over me! At best jumping about, and taking all the attention I had! No, thank you!"

"Come, George," said his sister, "you will make them think you are no horseman!"

"I am not, and you know it! I am not going to make a fool of myself on compulsion! I know what I can do, and what I can't do."

"I wish I had the chance!" murmured Walter, as if to himself, but so that Lufa heard.

"You can ride?" asked Lufa, with pleased surprise.

"Why not?" returned Walter. "Every Englishman should ride."

"Yes, every Englishman should swim, but Englishmen are drowned every day!"

"That is often because they can swim, but have not Mr. Sefton's prudence."

"You mustn't think my cousin is afraid of Red Racket!" she returned.

"I don't. He doesn't look like it."

"Do you really wish to ride the roan?"

"Indeed I do!"

"I will order him round," she said, rising.

Walter did not quite enjoy her consenting so easily; had she no fear for him of the risk Mr. Sefton would not run?

"She wants me to cut a good figure!" he said to himself, and went to get ready.

There is no deed of prowess on Walter's part to record. The instant he was in the saddle, Red Racket recognized a master.

"You can't have ridden him before?" questioned Lufa.

"I never saw him till this morning."

"He likes you, I suppose!" she said.

As they returned, the other ladies being in front, and the groom some distance behind, Walter brought his roan side by side with Lufa's horse, and said, "You know Browning's 'Last Ride Together'?"

"Yes," she answered, with a faint blush, "but this is not our last ride! It is our first! Why didn't you tell me? We might have had many rides together!"

"Promise me a last one," he said.

"How can I? How should I know it was the last?"

"Promise," he persisted, "that if ever you see just one last ride possible, you will let me know."

She hesitated a moment, then answered, "I will."

"Thank you!" said Walter with fervor.

As by consent, they rode after the others.

Walter had not yet the courage to say anything definite of his love to Lufa. But he had said many things that must have compelled her to imagine what he had not said; therefore, the promise she had given him seemed encouraging. They rode in silence the rest of the way.

When Sefton saw Red Racket as quiet as a lamb, he went up to him, stroked his neck, and said to Walter, "With me he would have capered like an idiot till he had thrown me. It is always luck with horses of his color! You must have a light hand!"

He stroked his neck once more, turned aside, and was too late to help the ladies dismount.

It was the last ride for the present, because of a change in the

72

weather. In a few days *The Field Battery* came with Walter's review, bringing a revival of the self-reproach he had begun to forget. In his hand, the paper felt like bad news or something nasty. He could not bear the thought of having to take his part in the talk it would occasion. It could not now be helped, however, and that was a great comfort! It was impossible, nonetheless, to keep it up. As he had foreseen, all this time came no revival of his first impression of the poem.

He went to find his hostess, and told her he must go to London that same afternoon. As he took his leave, he put the paper in Lufa's hand, saying, "You will find there what I have said about the poem."

Chapter 19.

WALTER'S FIRSTBORN

Back in Lufa-less London, Walter found his first lonely evening dull. He was not yet capable of looking beneath the look of anything. He felt cabined, cribbed, confined. His world-clothing came too near him. From the flowing robes of a park, a great house—large rooms, wide staircases, plenty of air and space, color, softness, fitness, and completeness—he found himself in the worn, tight, shabby garment of a cheap London lodging!

But Walter, far from being a wise man, was not therefore a fool; he was not one whom this world cannot teach. No man is a fool who, having work to do, sets himself to do it. Walter had begun a poem to lead the van of a volume, of which the rest was nearly ready; into it he now set himself to weave a sequel to Lufa's poetic drama, from the point where she had left the story. Every hour he could spare from drudgery he devoted to it, urged by the delightful prospect of letting Lufa see what he could do. Gaining power with his stanza as he went on, the pleasure of it grew and more than comforted his loneliness. Sullivan could hardly get him from his room.

Walter found a young publisher prepared to undertake half the risk, on the unexpressed ground of the author's proximity to the judgment seat. Walter was too experienced to look for any gain; yet he hoped to clear his expenses, and so became liable for much more than he possessed.

He had one little note from Lufa, concerning a point in rhythm which perplexed her. She had a good ear, and was

74

conscientious in her mechanics. There was not a cockney rhyme from beginning to end in her poem, which is more than the uninitiated will count worthy. But she understood nothing of the broken music which a master of verse will turn to such high service. There are lines in Milton which Walter, who knew far more than she, could not read well until long after, when Dante taught him how.

In the month of December came another note from Lady Lufa, inviting him to spend a week with them after Christmas.

"Perhaps then we may have yet a ride together," added a postscript.

"What does she mean?" thought Walter, a pale fear at his heart. "She cannot mean one last ride!"

One conclusion he came to—he must tell her plainly that he loved her. The thing was only right, though of course ridiculous in the eyes of worldly people, or so thought the far-from-unworldy poet. True, she was the daughter of an earl, and he the son of a farmer; and those who called the land their own looked down upon those who tilled it! But a banker or a brewer, or the son of a man who had wielded the spade might marry an earl's daughter; why should not the son of a farmer, and one who, according to the lady's mother, himself belonged to an aristocracy? The farmer's son indeed was poor, and who would look at a poor banker or a poor brewer more than a poor farmer? It was all money! But was he going to give in to that? Was he to grant that possession made a man honorable, and the want of it despicable? To act as if she could think after such a silly fashion would be to insult her! He would lay bare his heart to her! There were things in it which she knew what value to set upon—things as far before birth as birth was before money! He would accept the invitation and, if possible, get his volume out before the day mentioned. So, he hoped, to be a little in the mouth of the public when he went.

Walter, like many another youth, imagined the way to make a woman love him was to humble himself before her, to tell her how beautiful she was and how much he loved her. But why should any woman therefore love a man? If she loves him already, anything will do to make her love him more; if she does not, no entreaty will wake what is not there to be waked. Even wrong and cruelty and carelessness may increase love already rooted; but neither love nor kindness nor worship will prevail to plant it.

In his formal acceptance of the invitation, he enclosed some verses destined for his volume, in which he poured out his boyish passion over his lady's hair and eyes and hands—a poem not without some of the merits made much of by the rising school of the day, and possessing qualities higher, perhaps, than those upon which that school chiefly prided itself. She made, and he expected, no acknowledgment, but she did not return the verses.

Lyric after lyric, with Lufa for its inspiration, he wrought, like damask flowers, into his poem. Every evening, he fashioned and filed, until at length it was finished.

When the publisher's girl appeared with the proof sheets in her hand, she came like a winged ministrant laying a wondrous gift before him. And in truth, poor as he came to think it, was it not truly a gift greater than any angel could have brought him? Was not the seed of it sown in his being by Him that loved him before he was? These were the poor first flowers, come to make way for better, themselves a gift none but God could give.

The book was rapidly approaching its birth, as the day of Lufa's summons drew near. He had inscribed the volume to her—not by name, but in a dedication she could not but understand and no other would, founded on her promise of a last ride. It was so delightful to have a secret with her! He hoped to the last moment to take a copy with him, but was disappointed by a mishap with the binding—about which he was as particular as if it had been itself a poem—and so he had to pack without it.

On his way to the station, he kept repeating to himself, "Is it to be the last ride, or only another?"

Chapter 20.

A BLOSSOM IN WINTER

When Walter arrived, he found the paradise under snow. But the summer had only run indoors and was blooming there. Lufa was kinder than ever, but, he fancied, a little embarrassed, which he interpreted to his advantage. He was shown to the room he had before occupied.

It did not take him long to learn the winter ways of the house. Mr. Sefton and his sister were there, and all seemed glad of his help against consciousness. There could be no riding so long as the frost lasted and the snow kept falling, and the ladies did not care to go out. In some country houses, Time has as many lives as a cat and wants a great deal of killing—a butchery to be one day bitterly repented perhaps. But as a savage cannot be a citizen, so people of fashion cannot belong to the kingdom of heaven.

The third morning came a thaw, with a storm of wind and rain, and after lunch they gathered in the glooming library and began to tell ghost stories. Walter happened to know a few of the rarer sort, and found himself in his element. His art came to help him, as did the eyes of the ladies, and he rose to his best. As Walter was working one of his tales to its climax, Mr. Sefton entered the room and took a chair beside Lufa, who had momentarily dropped her needlework.

She rose, saying, "I beg your pardon, Mr. Colman, but would you mind stopping a minute while I get a little more red silk for my imperial dragon? Mr. Sefton has already taken the sting out of the snake!"

"What snake?" asked Sefton.

"The snake of terror," she answered. "Did you not see him as you came in—erect on his coiled tail, drawing his head back for his darting spring?"

"I am very sorry," said Sefton. "I have injured all present, and I hope all will pardon me!"

When Lufa had found her silk, she took a seat nearer to Walter, who resumed and finished his narrative.

"I wonder she lived to tell it!" said one of the ladies.

"For my part," rejoined their hostess, "I do not see why everyone should be so terrified at the thought of meeting a ghost! It seems to me cowardly."

"I don't think it cowardly," said Sefton, "to be frightened at a ghost, or at anything else."

"Now don't say you would run away!" remonstrated his sister.

"I couldn't very well if I was in bed! But I might hide my head under the blankets!"

"I don't believe it a bit!"

"To be sure," continued Sefton reflectively, "there does seem a difference! To hide is one thing, and to run is another—quite another thing! If you are frightened, you are frightened and you can't help it; but if you run away, then you are a coward. Yes—quite true! And yet there are things some men, whom other men would be afraid to call cowards, would run from fast enough! Your story, Mr. Colman," he went on, "reminds me of an adventure I had—if that be an adventure where there was no danger—except, indeed, of losing my wits, which Lufa would say was no great loss. I don't often tell the story, for I have an odd way of being believed—and nobody ever does believe that story, though it is as true as I live. But when a thing is true, the blame lies with those that don't believe it. Are you not of my mind, Mr. Colman?"

"You had better not appeal to him!" said Lufa. "Mr. Colman does not believe a word of the stories he has been telling. He regards them entirely from the artistic point of view, and cares only for their effect. He is writing a novel, and wants to study people under a ghost story."

"I don't endorse your judgment of me, Lady Lufa," said Walter, who did not quite believe what she said. "I am ready to believe anything in which I can see reason. I should much like to hear Mr. Sefton's story. I never met the man who saw a ghost, unless Mr. Sefton is that man."

"You shall say what you will when you have heard. I shall offer no explanation. I shall only tell you what I saw, or, if you prefer it, experienced; you must then fall back on your own metaphysics. I don't care what anybody thinks about it."

"You are not very polite!" said Lufa.

"Only truthful," replied Sefton.

"Please go on."

"We are dying to hear."

"A real ghost story!"

"Is it your best, George?"

"It is my only one," Sefton answered, and was silent a few moments, as if arranging his thoughts. "I was staying at a country house," he began. "I have reasons for not saying where it was, or where it wasn't. It may have been in Ireland, it may have been in Scotland, it may have been in England; it was one of the three—an old house, in parts *very* old. One morning I happened to sleep late, and found the breakfast table deserted. I was not the last, however, for presently another man appeared, whom I had met at dinner the day before for the first time. I knew he had passed an uncomfortable night, for his face was like dough, with livid spots under his eyes. He sat down and poured himself out a cup of tea.

" 'Game pie?' I said, but he did not heed me. There was nobody in the room but ourselves, and I thought it best to leave him alone.

" 'Are you an old friend of the family?' he said at length.

" 'About the age of most friends,' I answered.

"He was silent again for a bit, then said, 'I'm leaving this horrible house! Not another moment will I stay!'

" 'Pray don't imagine I want to know why,' I replied.

" 'Neither do I want to tell,' he rejoined. 'I don't care to have fellows laugh at me!'

" 'That's just what I don't care to do. Nothing hurts me more than being laughed at, so I take no pleasure in it,' I said.

" 'What I do want,' said he, 'is to have you tell our hostess why I went.'

" 'Very well, I will. Why are you going?'

" 'Can't you help a fellow to an excuse? I'm not going to give *her* the reason.'

" 'Tell me what you want me to say, and I will tell her you told me to say so.'

" 'I will tell *you* the truth.'

" 'Fire away, then.'

" 'I was in a beastly funk last night. I dare say you think as I did, that a man ought never to be a hair off the cool?'

" 'That depends,' I replied. 'There are some things, and there may be more, at which any but an idiot might well be scared— but some are such fools they can't shiver! What's the matter? I give you my word I'll not make game of it.'

" 'Well,' he said, 'I will tell you. Last night, I had been in bed about five minutes, and hadn't even had time to grow sleepy, when I heard a curious shuffling in the passage outside my door, and an indescribable terror came over me. To be perfectly open with you, however, I *had* heard that was the sign she was coming!'

" '*Who* coming?'

" 'The ghost, of course!'

" 'The ghost!'

" 'You don't mean to say you never heard of the ghost?'

" 'Never heard a word of it.'

" 'Well, they don't like to speak of it, but everybody knows!' He went on, but plainly with a tearing effort. 'The shuffling was like feet in slippers much too big. As if I had been five instead of five-and-thirty, I dived under the blankets, and lay so for minutes after the shuffling had ceased. But at length I persuaded myself it was but a foolish fancy, and that I had never really heard anything. What with fear and heat I was much in want of breath too, I can tell you! So I came to the surface, and looked out.' Here he paused a moment, and turned almost livid. 'There stood a horrible old woman, staring at me, as if she had been seeing me all the time, and the blankets made no difference!'

" 'Was she really ugly?' I asked.

" 'Well, I don't know what you call ugly,' he answered, 'but if you had seen her stare, you would have thought her ugly enough! Had she been as beautiful as a maiden of paradise, though, I don't imagine I should have been less frightened! I cannot tell what came next. I came to myself all trembling, and

80

as cold and as wet as if I had been dipped in a well.'

" 'You are sure you were not dreaming?' I said.

" 'I was not! But I do not expect you to believe me!'

" 'You must not be offended,' I said, 'if I find the thing stiff to stow! I believe *you* all the same.'

" 'What?' he said, not quite understanding me.

" 'An honest man and a gentleman,' I answered.

" 'And a coward to boot!'

" 'God forbid!' I returned. 'What man can answer for himself at every moment? If I remember, Hector turned at last and ran from Achilles!'

"Then he drank his cup of tea, got up, and said, 'I'm off. Good-bye—and thank you! A million pounds wouldn't make me stay in the house another hour! There is that in it I fear ten times worse than the ghost!'

" 'Gracious! What is that?'

" 'This horrible cowardice oozing from her like a mist. The house is full of it!'

" 'But what shall I say to our hostess?'

" 'Anything you like!'

" 'I will say then, that you are very sorry, but were compelled to go.'

" 'Say what you please, only let me go! Tell them to send my traps after me. Good-bye!'

"So he went."

"And what became of him?"

"I've neither seen nor heard of him to this day!"

He ceased with the cadence of an ended story.

"Is that all? You spoke of an adventure of your own! I was flattering myself," said Lufa, "that in our house Mr. Colman was at last to hear a ghost story from the man's own lips!"

"The sun is coming out!" said Sefton. "I will have a cigar at the stables."

The company protested, but he turned a deaf ear to expostulation, and went out.

Chapter 21.

THE BODILESS

In the drawing room after dinner, some of the ladies gathered about Sefton, and begged the story of his own adventure. He smiled oddly, and answered, "Very well, you shall have it!"

They seated themselves, and the company came from all parts of the room—among the rest, Lufa and Walter.

"It was three days after my friend left," began Sefton, "when one night I found myself alone in the drawing room, just waked from a brown study. No one had said good-night to me. I looked at my watch; it was half-past eleven. I rose and headed for my bedroom in the second floor.

"The stairs were peculiar—a construction later than much of the house, but by no means modern. When you reached the landing of the second floor and looked up, you could see above you the third floor, defended by a balustrade between arches. There were no carpets on stairs or landings, which were all of oak.

"I cannot certainly say what made me look up; but I am almost sure I heard a noise like that the ghost was said to make, as of one walking in shoes too large. Then I saw a lady looking down over the balustrade on the third floor. I thought someone was playing me a trick, and imitating the ghost, for the ladies had been chaffing me a good deal that night. She wore an old-fashioned, silky brown dress. I rushed up to see who was taking the rise out of me. I looked up at her as I ran, and she kept looking down, but apparently not at me. Her face was that of a middle-aged woman, beginning, indeed, to be old, and had an intent, rather troubled look.

"I was at the top in a moment, on the level where she stood leaning over the handrail. I approached her, but apparently she neither saw nor heard me. 'Well acted!' I said to myself, but even then I was beginning to be afraid, without knowing why. Every man's impulse, I fancy, is to go right up to anything that frightens him—at least, I have always found it so. I walked close up to the woman. She moved her head and turned in my direction, but only as if to go away. Whether she looked at me I cannot tell, but I saw her eyes plainly enough. By this time, I suppose, the idea of a ghost must have been uppermost, for, being now quite close to her, I put out my hand as if to touch her. *My hand went through her—through her head and body!* I am not joking in the least. I mean you to believe, if you can, exactly what I say. What then she did, or whether she took any notice of my movement, I cannot tell; I only know what *I* did, or rather what I did not do. For, had I been capable, I should have uttered a shriek that would have filled the house with ghastly terror; but there was a load of iron on my chest, and the hand of a giant at my throat. I could not help opening my mouth, for something drew all the muscles of my jaws and throat, but I could not utter a sound. The horror I was in was entirely new to me, and no more under my control than a fever. I only wonder it did not paralyze me, that I was able to turn and run down the stair! I ran as if all the cardinal sins were at my heels. I flew, never seeming to touch the stairs as I went. I darted along the passage, burst into my room, shut and locked the door, lighted my candles, fell into a chair, shuddered, and began to breathe again."

He ceased, not without present signs of the agitation he described.

"And what else?" asked one of the company.

"Did anything happen?" demanded another.

"Do tell us more!" pleaded a third.

"I have nothing more to *tell*," answered Sefton. "But I haven't done *wondering*. What could have put me in such an awful funk? Why should anyone have been terrified? The poor thing had lost her body, it is true, but there she was all the same! It might be nicer or not so nice to her, but why should it so affect me? That's what I want to know! Am I not, as Hamlet says, 'a thing immortal as itself'? I don't see the sense of it! Sure I am that one meets constantly—sits down with, eats and drinks with, hears sing and play and remark on the weather and the fate of the nation—"

He paused, his eyes fixed on Walter.

"What *are* you driving at?" said Lufa.

"I was thinking of a much more fearful kind of creature," he answered.

"What kind of creature?" she asked.

"A creature," he said slowly, "that has a body, but no soul. All body, with brain enough for its affairs, yet it has no soul. Such will never wander about after they are dead! There will be nothing to wander! Good night, ladies! Were I to tell you the history of a woman whose acquaintance I made some years ago, you would understand the sort. Good night!"

There was silence for a moment or two. Had not his sister been present, something other than complimentary to Sefton might have crept about the drawing room—to judge from the expression on two or three faces. Walter felt the man worth knowing, but felt also something repellent about him.

Chapter 22.

THE SOULLESS

In his room, Walter threw himself in a chair and sat without thinking, for the mental presence of Lufa was hardly thought. Gradually Sefton's story revived, and for a time displaced the image of Lufa. It was the first immediately authenticated ghost narration he had ever heard. His fancy alone had always been attracted by such tales, but this one brought him close to things of import both profound and marvelous. He began to wonder how he was likely to carry himself in such an encounter. Courage such as Mr. Sefton's he dared not claim—anymore than he could hope for the distinction of ever putting his hand through a ghost! The ghost, he held, never saw Sefton, knew or thought of his presence, or was aware of any intrusive outrage from his hand! Walter shrank nonetheless, however, from such a phantasmic presence as Sefton had described; a man's philosophy made but a fool of him when it came to the pinch! He would indeed like to see a ghost, but not to be alone with one!

Then he remembered a certain look on Lufa's face, which he had not then understood; was it possible she knew something about the thing? Could this be the house where the ghost appeared? The room in which he sat was very old, and but for their age, none of the pictures would be hung upon any wall! And the huge gloomy bed on the third floor too! What if this was the very room the officer slept in?

Walter longed to run into port, to find shelter from the terrors of the shoreless sea of the unknown. But the only harbor he could seek was bed and closed eyes! The dark is a strange

85

refuge from the darkness, and yet is that which most men seek. It is so dark—yet they go further from the light! Thus deeper they go, and come upon greater terrors. He undressed hurriedly, blew out his candles, and by the light of the fire, glowing now rather than blazing, plunged into the expanse which glimmered before him like a lake of sleep in the moonshine of dreams.

The moment he laid down his head, he became aware of what seemed an unnatural stillness. Throughout the evening a strong wind had been blowing about the house, but now it had ceased. Without having noted the tumult, Walter was aware of the calm. But what made him so cold? The surface of the linen was like a film of ice! He rolled himself round, and like a hedgehog sought shelter within the circumference of his own person, but he could not get warm. Had the room turned suddenly cold? Could the ghost be near, making the air like that of the sepulchre from which she had just issued? For such ghosts as walk the world at night, what refuge is so fit in the daytime as their tombs? The thought was a worse horror than he had known himself capable of feeling. He shivered with the cold. It seemed to pierce his very bones, and a strange and hideous constriction seized the muscles of his neck and throat. Had not Sefton described the sensation? Was it not a sure sign of the ghostly presence?

Had Molly been in like predicament, she would have found immediate refuge with Him to whom belong all ghosts, wherever they roam or rest—with Him who can deliver from the terrors of the night as well as from the perplexities of the day. But Walter felt his lonely being exposed on all sides.

The handle of the door moved. Ghosts may or may not enter and leave a room in silence, but the sound shook Walter's nerves horribly, and nearly made an end of him.

But then Sefton's voice said, "May I come in?" and Walter's terror subsided. Sefton opened the door wider, entered, closed it softly, and approached the bed through the dull firelight. "I did not think you would be in bed!" he said. "But at the risk of waking you, even of giving you a sleepless night, I must have a little talk with you!"

"I shall be glad," answered Walter.

Sefton little knew how welcome his visit was!

But he had come to do Walter a service for which he could hardly at once be grateful. The best things done for any are generally those for which they are at the moment least grateful; it needs the result of the service to make them able to prize it.

Walter thought he had more of the story to tell—something he had not chosen to relate to the ladies.

Sefton stood, and for a few moments there was silence. He seemed to be meditating, yet looked like one who wanted to light his cigar.

"Won't you take a seat?" said Walter.

"Thank you!" returned Sefton, and sat on the bed. "I am twenty-seven," he said at length. "How old are you?"

"Twenty-three," answered Walter.

"When I was twenty-three, I knew ever so much more than I do now! I'm not half so sure about things as I was. I wonder if you will find it so."

"I hope I shall—otherwise I shan't have got on."

"Well now, couldn't you just forestall your experience by making use of mine? Look here, Mr. Colman! I like you, and believe you will one day be something more than a gentleman. But I must tell you that you're on the wrong tack here, old boy!"

"I'm sorry—I don't understand you," said Walter.

"Naturally not. How could you? I will explain. You heard my story about the ghost?" said Sefton.

"I was on the point of asking you if I might tell it in print!"

"You may do what you like with it, except the other fellow's part."

"Thank you. But I wish you would tell me what you meant by that other more fearful—apparition—or what did you call it? Were you alluding to the vampire?"

"No. There are live women worse than vampires. Scared as I confess I was, I would rather meet ten such ghosts as I told you of, than another woman such as I mean. I know one, and she's enough. By the time you had seen ten ghosts you would have got used to them, and found there was no danger from them; but a woman without a soul will devour any number of men. She's all room inside! Look here! I must be open with you. Tell me you are not in love with my cousin Lufa and I will bid you good-night."

"I am so much in love with her, that I dare not think what may come of it," replied Walter.

"Then tell her, man, and have done with it! Anything will be better than going on like this. I will not say what Lufa is; indeed, I don't know what name would be at all fit for her! You think me a dry, odd sort of customer? I was different when I fell in love with Lufa. She is older than you think her, though not so old as I am. I kept saying to myself that she was hardly a woman yet, and I must give her time. I was better brought up than she; I thought things of consequence that she thought of none. I hadn't a stupid ordinary mother like hers. She's my second cousin. She took all my love words, never drew me on, never pushed me back, never refused my love, never returned it. Whatever I did or said, she seemed content.

"She was always writing poetry. 'But where's her own poetry?' I would ask myself. I was always trying to get nearer to what I admired; she never seemed to suspect the least relation between the ideal and life, between thought and action. To have an ideal implied no aspiration after it! She has not a thought of the smallest obligation to carry out one of the fine things she writes of, any more than most people who go to church think they have anything to do with what they hear there.

"Most people's nature seems all in pieces. They wear and change their moods as they wear and change their dresses. Their moods make them, and not they their moods. They are different with every different mood. But Lufa seems never to change, and yet never to be in one and the same mood. She is always in two moods, and the one mood has nothing to do with the other. The one mood never influences, never modifies the other. They run side by side and do not mingle. The one mood is enthusiasm for what is not, while the other mood is indifference to what is. She has no faintest desire to make what is not into what is. As for love, she believes it a fine thing to be loved. She loves nobody but her mother, and her only after a fashion. I had my leg broken in the hunting field once, and my horse got up and galloped off while I lay still. She saw what had happened and sent after the hounds. She said she could do no good; Dr. Black was in the field, and she went to find him. She didn't find him, and he didn't come. I believe she forgot. But it's worth telling you, though it has nothing to do with her, that

I wasn't forgotten. Old Truefoot went straight home, and kept wheeling and tearing up and down before the windows; but, till his old groom came, he would let no one touch him. Then when the groom would have led him to the stable, he set his forefeet out in front of him, and wouldn't budge. The groom got on his back, but was scarcely in the saddle when Truefoot was off in a beeline over everything to where I was lying. There's a horse for you! And there's a woman! I'm telling you all this, mind, not to blame her, but to warn you. Whether she is liable for blame or not, I don't know, for I don't understand her.

"I was free to come and go and say what I pleased, for both families favored the match. She never objected, never said she would not have me, and even said she liked me as well as any other. In a word she would have married me, if I would have taken her. There are men, I believe, who would make the best of such a consent, saying they were so in love with the woman they would rejoice to take her on any terms. I don't understand that sort of love! I would as soon think of marrying a woman I hated as a woman that did not love me. I know no reason why any woman should love me, and if no woman can find any, I must go alone. Lufa has found none yet, and life and love too seem to have gone out of me while I'm waiting. If you ask me why I do not give it all up, I have no answer.

"You will say for Lufa, it is only that the right man is not come! It may be so; but I believe there is more than that in it. I fear she is all outside. It is true her poetry is even passionate sometimes, but I suspect all her inspiration comes of the poetry she reads, not of the nature or human nature around her; it comes of ambition, not of love. I don't know much about verse, but to me there is an air of artificiality about all hers. I cannot understand how you could praise her long poem so much if you loved her.

"She has grown to me like the ghost I told you of. I put out my hand to her, and it goes through her. It makes me feel dead myself to be with her. I wonder sometimes how it would be if suddenly she said she loved me. Should I love her, or should we have changed parts? She is very dainty, very ladylike—but womanly? At one time—and for this I am now punished—the ambition to wake love in her had no small part in my feeling toward her: ambition to be the first and only man so to move her! Despair has long cured me of that, but not before I had come to love her in a way I cannot now understand. Why I should love her I cannot tell; and were it not that I scorn to marry her without love, I should despise my very love.

"You are thinking, 'Well then, the way is clear for me!' It is. I only want to prepare you for what I am confident will follow—you will have the heart taken out of you! That you are poor will be little obstacle if she loves you. She is an heiress and can do much as she pleases. If she were in love, she would be obstinate. It must be in her somewhere, you will say, else how could she write as she does? But, I say again, look at the multitudes who go to church and communicate, with whose beings religion has no more to do than with that of Satan! Well, I've said my say, and so, good night!"

He rose and stood. He had not uttered the depth of what he feared concerning Lufa—that she was simply, unobtrusively, unconsciously, absolutely selfish.

Walter had listened with a beating heart, now full of hope that he was *the man* for this woman, now sick with the conviction that he was destined to fare no better than Sefton.

"Let me have my say before you go," Walter protested. "It will sound as presumptuous in your ears as it does in mine—but what is to be done except put the thing to the question?"

"There is nothing else. That is all I want. You must not go on like this. It is sucking the life out of you, and I can't bear to see it. Pray do not misunderstand me."

"That is impossible," returned Walter. "I can only go on."

Not a wink did he sleep that night. But ever and again across his anxiety, throughout the dark hours, came the flattering thought that she had never yet loved a man, but he was teaching her to love. He did not doubt Sefton, but Sefton might be right only for himself.

Chapter 23.

THE LAST RIDE?

In the morning, as Walter was dressing, he received a copy of his poems which he had taken in sheets to a bookbinder to put in moroccan leather for Lady Lufa. Pleased like a child, he handled it as if he might hurt it. Such a feeling he had never had before, would never have again. He was an author! One might think, after the way in which he had treated not a few books and not a few authors, he could scarcely consider it such a very fine thing to be an author; but the difference between thine and mine is always treated by the man of this world as essential. The book was Walter's and not another's! No common prose or poetry this, but the firstborn of his deepest feeling! It had taken body and shape; from the unseen it had emerged in red morocco, the color of his heart, it edges golden with the light of his hopes.

As to the communication of the night, its pain had nearly vanished. Was not Sefton a disappointed lover? His honesty, however evident, could not alter that fact! Least of all could a man himself tell whether disguised jealousy and lingering hope might not be potently present, while he believed himself solely influenced by friendly anxiety.

"I will take his advice, however," said Walter to himself, "and put an end to my anxiety this very day!"

"Do you feel inclined for a gallop, Mr. Colman?" asked Lufa as they sat at the breakfast table. "It feels just like a spring morning. The wind changed in the night. You won't mind a little mud, will you?"

With a common phrase, but with a foolish look of adoring gratitude, Walter accepted the invitation. "How handsome he is!" thought Lufa, for Walter's countenance was not only handsome but expressive. Most women, however, found him attractive chiefly from his frank address and open look; for, though yet far from a true man, he was of a true nature. Every man's nature indeed is true, though the man may be not true; but some have come into the world so much nearer the point where they may begin to be true that, comparing them with the rest, we say their nature is true.

Lufa rose and went to get ready. Walter followed, and overtook her on the stair.

"I have something for you," he said. "May I bring it to you?"

He could not postpone the effect his book might have. Authors young and old think so much of their books that they seldom conceive how little others care about them.

She was hardly in her room, when he followed her with the volume. She took it and opened it. "Yours!" she cried. "And poetry! Why, Walter!" She had only once or twice before called him by his name.

He took it from her hand, and turning the title page, gave it to her again to read the dedication. A slight rose tinge suffused her face. She said nothing, but shut the book and gave it a tender little hug.

"She never did that to anything Sefton gave her!" thought Walter.

"Make haste," she said, and turning, went in and closed her door.

He walked up and down the hall for half an hour before she appeared. Then she came tripping down the wide, softly descending stair, in her tight-fitting habit, and hat and feather, holding up her skirt, so that he saw her feet racing each other like a little cataract across the steps. She said as she came near him, "I have kept you waiting, but I could not help it; my habit was torn!" He thought he had never seen her so lovely. Indeed, she looked lovely, and had she loved, would have been lovely. As it was, her outer loveliness was but a promise whose fulfillment had been too long postponed. His heart swelled into his throat and eyes as he followed her, and helped her to mount.

"Nobody puts me up so well as you!" she said.

92

He could hardly repress the triumph that filled him from head to foot. Anyhow, and whoever might object, she liked him! If she loved him and would confess it, he could live on the pride of it all the rest of his days!

They were unattended, but neither spoke until they were well beyond the lodge gate. Winter though it was, a sweet air was all abroad, and the day was full of spring prophecies; all winters have such days, even those of the heart! How else could we get through them? Their horses were in excellent spirits, in their first gallop for more than a week, and Walter's roan was like a flame under him. The horses gave them so much to do that no such talk as Walter longed for was possible. It consoled him, however, to think that he had never had such a chance of letting Lufa see how he could ride.

At length, after a great gallop, their mounts were quieter, seeming to remember they were horses and not colts, and must not overpass the limits of equine propriety.

"Is it our last ride, Lufa?" said Walter.

"Why should it be?" she answered, opening her eyes wide on him.

"There is no reason I know," he returned, "unless—unless you are tired of me."

"Nobody is tired of you—except perhaps George, and you need not mind him; he is odd. I have known him from childhood, and I don't understand him yet."

"He is clever!" said Walter.

"I dare say he is—if he would take the trouble to show it."

"You hardly do him justice, I think!"

"How can I? He bores me! And when I am bored, I am terribly bored. I have been very patient with him."

"Why do you ask him so often then?"

"*I* don't ask him. Mamma is fond of him, and so—"

"You are the victim!"

"I can bear it; I have consolations!" she laughed merrily.

"How do you like my binding?" he asked, when they had ridden a while in silence.

She looked up with a question.

"The binding of my book, I mean," he explained.

"It is a good color."

He felt his hope rather dampened. "Will you let me read you

93

a little from it?"

"With pleasure. You shall have an audience in the drawing room, after luncheon."

"O Lufa! How could you think I would read my own poems to a lot of people?"

"I beg your pardon! Will the summerhouse do?"

"Yes, indeed—nowhere better."

"Very well! The summerhouse, after lunch!"

This was not encouraging! Did she suspect what was coming? And was she careful not to lead the way to it? She had never been like this before. Perhaps she did not like having the book dedicated to her—but there was no mention of her name, or anything to let "the heartless world" know to whom it was offered.

As they approached the house, Walter said, "Would you mind coming at once to the summerhouse?"

"Lunch will be ready."

"Then sit down in your habit, and come immediately after. Let me have my way for once, Lufa."

"Very well."

Chapter 24

THE SUMMERHOUSE

The moment the meal was over, Walter left the room, and in five minutes met Lufa at the place appointed—a building like a miniature Roman temple.

"Oh," said Lufa as she entered. "I forgot the book! How stupid of me!"

"Never mind," returned Walter. "It was you, not the book I wanted."

A broad bench went round the circular wall. Lufa seated herself on it, and Walter placed himself beside her, as near as he dared. For some moments he did not speak. She looked up at him inquiringly. He sank at her feet, bowed his head toward her, and but for lack of courage would have laid it on her knees.

"O Lufa!" he said, "you cannot think how much I love you!"

"Poor, dear boy!" she returned, in the tone of a careless mother to whom a son has unburdened his sorrows, and she laid her hand lightly on his curls. The words were not repellent, but neither was the tone encouraging.

"You do not mind my saying it?" he resumed, feeling his way timidly.

"What could you do but tell me?" she answered. "What could I do for you if you did not let me know! I'm *so* sorry, Walter!"

"Why should you be sorry? You can do with me as you please!"

"I don't know about such things. I don't quite know what you mean, or what you want. I will be as kind to you as I can—while you stay with us."

"But, Lufa—I may call you Lufa?"

"Yes, surely, if that is any comfort to you."

"Nothing but your love, Lufa, can be a comfort to me. That would make me one of the blessed."

"I like you very much. If you were a girl, I should have said I loved you."

"Why not say it as it is?"

"Would you be content with the love I should give a girl? Some of you men want so much!"

"I will be glad of any love you can give me. But to say I should be content with *any* love you could give me would be false. My love to you is such that I don't know how to bear it! It aches so! My heart is full of you, and longs for you till I can hardly endure the pain. You are so beautiful that your beauty burns me. Neither night nor day can I forget you!"

"You try to forget me then?"

"Never. Your eyes have so dazzled my soul that I can see nothing but your eyes. Do look at me—just for one moment, Lufa."

She turned her face and looked him straight in the eyes—looked into them as if they were windows through which she could peer into the convolutions of his brain. She held her eyes steady until his dropped, unable to sustain the nearness of her presence.

"You see," she said, "I am ready to do anything I can to please you!"

He felt strangely defeated. He rose and sat down beside her again, with the sickness of a hot summer noon in his soul. But he must leave no room for mistake! He had been dreaming long enough!

"Is it possible you do not understand, Lufa, what a man means when he says, 'I love you'?"

"I think I do! I don't mind it!"

"That means you will love me also?"

"Yes, I will be good to you."

"You will love me as a woman loves a man?"

"I will let you love me as much as you please."

"To love you as much as I please would be to call you my own; to marry you; to say *wife* to you; to have you altogether, with nobody to come between, or try to stop my worshiping of you—not father, not mother, not anybody!"

"Now you are foolish, Walter! You know I never meant that! You must have known that never could be! I never imagined you could make such a fantastic blunder! But then how should you know how *we* think about things! I must remember that, and not be hard upon you!"

"You mean that your father and mother would not like it?"

"There it is! You do not understand! I thought so. I do not mean my father and mother in particular; I mean our people—people of our position. I would say *rank*, but that might hurt you. We are brought up so differently from you that you cannot understand how we think of such things. It grieves me to appear unkind, but really, Walter! There is not a man I love more than you—but marriage? *Lady Lufa* would be in everybody's mouth, the same as if I had run off with my groom! Believe me, our people are so blind that they would hardly see the difference. The thing is simply impossible!"

"It would not be impossible if you loved me!"

"Then I don't, never did, never could love you. Don't imagine you can persuade me to do anything unbecoming, anything treacherous to my people! You will find yourself awfully mistaken!"

"But I may make myself a name! If I were as famous as Lord Tennyson, would it be just as impossible?"

"To say it would not would be to confess myself worldly, and that I never was! No, Walter, I admire you. If you could be trusted not to misunderstand, I might even say I love you! I shall always be glad to see you, always enjoy hearing you read; but there is a line as impassable as the Persian river of death. Talk about something else or I must go!"

Here Walter, who had been shivering with cold, began to grow warm again as he answered. "How could you write that poem, Lady Lufa—full of such grand things about love, declaring love everything and rank nothing; and then, when it came to yourself, treat me like this? I could not have believed it possible! You cannot know what love is, however much you write about it!"

"I hope I never shall, if it means any confusion between friendship and folly! It shall not make a fool of *me!* I will *not* be talked about! It is all very well and very right in poetry! The idea of letting all go for love is so splendid, it is the greatest pity it should be impossible. There may be some planet whose social habits are different, where it might work well enough, but here it is not to be thought of—except in poetry, of course, or novels. Of all human relations, the idea of such love is certainly the fittest for verse; therefore, we have no choice—we must use it. But because I think with pleasure of such lovers, why must I consent to be looked at with pleasure myself? What obligation does my heroine lay on me to do likewise? I don't see the thing. I don't want to pose as a lover. Why should I fall in love with you in real life, because I like you to read my poem about lovers? Can't you see the absurdity of the argument? Life and books are two different spheres. The one is the sphere of thoughts, the other of things, and they don't touch."

But for pride, Walter could have wept with shame. Why should he care that one with such principles should grant or refuse him anything? Yet he did care!

"There is no reason at all," she resumed, "why we should not be friends. Mr. Colman, I am not a flirt. It is in my heart to be a sister to you! I would have you the first to congratulate me when the man appears whom I may choose to love as you mean! He need not be a poet to make you jealous. If he were, I should yet always regard you as my poet."

"And you would let me kiss your shoe, or perhaps your glove, if I was very good!" said Walter.

She took no notice of the outburst—it was but a bit of childish temper!

"You must learn," she went on, "to keep your life and your imagination apart. You are always letting them mix, and that confuses everything. A poet of all men ought not to make the mistake. It is quite monstrous! As monstrous as if a painter joined the halves of two different animals! Poetry is so unlike life that to carry the one into the other is to make the poet a ridiculous parody of a man! The moment that he plunges in, instead of standing aloof and regarding, he becomes a traitor to his art, and is no longer able to represent things as they ought to be but cannot. My mother and I will open to you the best doors in London because we like you; but pray, do not dream of more. Please, Walter, do leave it possible for me to say I like

98

you—oh, so much!"

She had been staring out the window as she spoke; now she turned her eyes upon him where he slumped beside her, crushed and broken. A breath of compassion seemed to ruffle the cold lake of her spirit, and she looked at him in silence for a moment. He did not raise his eyes, but her tone made her present to his whole being as she said, "I don't want to break your heart, my poet! It was a lovely thought—why did you spoil it?—that we two understood and loved each other in a way nobody could have a right to interfere with!"

Walter lifted his head. The word *loved* wrought on him like a spell: he was sadly a creature of words! He looked at her with flushed face and flashing eyes. Often had Lufa thought him handsome, but she had never felt it as she did now.

"Let it be so!" he said. "Be my sister-friend, Lufa. Leave it only to me to remember how foolish I once made myself in your beautiful eyes, how miserable always in my own blind heart."

So little of a man was our poet that out of pure disappointment and self-pity he burst into a passion of weeping. The world seemed lost to him, as it has seemed at such a time to many a better man. But to the true, the truth of things will sooner or later assert itself, and neither this world nor the next prove lost to him. A man's well-being does not depend on any woman. The woman did not create, and could not have contented him. No woman can ruin a man by refusing him, or even by accepting him, though she may go far toward it. There is One who has upon him a perfect claim, at the entrancing recognition of Whom he will one day cry out, "This, then, is what it all meant!" The lamp of poetry may for a time go out in the heart of the poet, and nature seem a blank; but where the truth is, the poetry must be; and truth *is*, however the untrue may fail to see it. Surely that man is a fool who, on the ground that there cannot be such a God as other fools assert, or such a God as alone he is able to imagine, says there is no God!

Lufa's bosom heaved, and she gave a little sob; her sentiment, the skin of her heart, was touched, for the thing was pathetic! A mist came over her eyes, and might, had she ever wept, have turned to tears.

Walter sat with his head in his hands and wept. She had

never before seen a man weep, yet never a tear left its heavenly spring to flow from her eyes! She rose, took his face between her hands, raised it, and kissed him on the forehead.

He rose also, suddenly calmed. "Then it *was* our last ride, Lufa!" he said, and left the summerhouse.

Chapter 25.

INTO THE PARK

Walter did not know where he was going when he turned from Lufa. It was solitude he sought, without being aware that he sought anything. Must it not be a deep spiritual instinct that drives trouble into solitude? There are times when only the Highest can comfort the lowest, and solitude is the antechamber to His presence. With Him is the only possibility of essential comfort, the comfort that turns an evil into a good. But it was certainly not *knowledge* of this that drove Walter into the wide, lonely park. "Away from men!" moans the wounded life. Away from the herd flies the wounded deer, away from the flock staggers the sickly sheep, to the solitary covert to die. The man too thinks he is to die; but he is in truth to return to life—if, indeed, he be a man, and not an abomination that can console himself with vile consolation. "You cannot soothe me, my friends! Leave me to my misery," cries the man; and lo, his misery is the wind of the waving garments of Him who walks in the garden in the cool of the day! All misery is *God unknown*.

Hurt and bleeding inside, Walter wandered away. His life was palled with a sudden hail-cloud which hung low and blotted out color and light and loveliness. It was afternoon, and the sun was fast going down. The dreary north wind had begun to blow, and the trees to moan in response, seeming to say, "How sad thou art, wind of winter! See how sad thou makest us! We moan and shiver! Each alone, we are sad!" The sorrow of nature was all about him, but the sighing of the wind-sifting trees around his head, and the hardening of the earth about the ancient roots under his feet, was better than the glow of the bright drawing room, with its lamps and blazing fires, its warm colors and caressing softnesses. Who would take joy in paradise with hell in his heart? Let him stay out in the night with the suffering, groaning trees, with the clouds that have swallowed the moon and the stars, with the frost and the silent gathering of the companies, troops, and battalions of snow!

Every man understands something of what Walter felt. His soul was seared with cold. The ways of life were a dull sickness. There was no reason why anything should be, why the world should ever have been made! The night was coming—why should he keep awake? How cold the river looked in its low, wet channel, and how listlessly the long grasses hung over its bank! And the boy on the other side was whistling!

It grew darker. He had made a long round and, unaware, approached the house. He had not thought what he must do. Nothing so practical as going away had yet occurred to him. She had not been unkind! She had even pressed on him a sister's love! The moth had not yet burned away enough of its wings to prevent it from burning its whole body, but kept fluttering about the flame. Nor was absent the childish weakness, the unmanly but common impulse, to make the woman feel how miserable she had made him. For this poor satisfaction not a few men have blown their brains out; not a few women drowned themselves, or taken poison—and generally without success.

Walter moved to go and stand before her the ruin she had made him, then vanish from her sight. Tomorrow he would leave the house, but she must see him alone yet once, before he went! Once more he must hang his shrivelled pinions in the presence of the seraph whose radiance had scorched him! And still the most hideous thought of all would keep lifting its vague ugly head out of chaos—the thought that, lovely as she was, she was not worshipful.

The windows were dimly shining through their thick curtains. The house looked a great jewel of bliss, in which the spirits of paradise might come and go, while such as he could not enter! What should he do? Where should he go? To his room and dress for dinner? It was impossible! How could he sit feeling her eyes, and facing Sefton! How could he endure the company, the talk, the horrible eating? All that had so lately been full of refinement, of enchantment—the music, the pictures, the easy chatter—all that was now stupid, wearisome, meaningless! He would go to his room and say he had a headache. But first he would peep into the drawing room, for *she* might be there, looking sad!

Chapter 26.

THE DRAWING ROOM

He opened a door into one of the smaller compartments of the drawing room, looked, crept in, and closed the door behind him.

Lufa was there—alone! He dared not approach her, but if he seated himself in a certain corner, he could see her and she him! He did not, however, realize that the corner he had chosen was entirely in shadow, or reflect that the globe of a lamp was almost directly between them. He thought she saw him, but she did not.

The room seemed to fold him round with softness as he entered from the dreary night, and he could not help being pervaded by the warmth, and weakened by the bodily comfort.

He sat up and gazed at his goddess—a mere idol, seeming, not being, until he hardly knew whether she was actually before him, or only present to his thought. She was indeed a little pale, but that she always was when quiet. No sorrow or shadow showed on her face. She seemed brooding, but over nothing painful. At length she smiled.

"She is pleased to think I love her!" thought Walter. "She leans to me a little! When the gray hair and the wrinkles come, it will be a gracious memory that she was so loved by one who had but his life to give her! 'He was poor,' she will say, 'but I have not found the riches he would have given me! I have been greatly loved!' "

Yet she was only meditating upon a verse that had come to her in the summerhouse, while Walter was weeping by her side.

A door opened, and Sefton came in. "Have you seen the *Onlooker?*" he asked, of a journal much in favor at the time with the more educated populace. "There is a review in it that would amuse you."

"Of what?" she asked listlessly.

"I didn't notice the name of the book, but it is a poem, and just your sort, I should say. The article is in the *Onlooker*'s best style."

"Pray let me see it!" she answered, holding out her hand.

"I will read it to you, if I may."

She did not object. He sat down a little way from her, and began to read. He had not gone far before Walter knew, although its name had not occurred as Sefton read, that the book was his own. The discovery enraged him—how had the reviewer got hold of it when he himself had seen no copy except Lufa's? It was a puzzle he never got at the root of. Probably someone he had offended had contrived to see as much of it, at the printer's or binder's, as had enabled him to forestall its appearance with the most stinging, mocking, playfully insolent paper that had ever rejoiced the readers of the *Onlooker*. But he had more to complain of than rudeness, a thing of which I doubt if any reviewer is aware. For he soon found that, by the blunder of the reviewer or printer, the best of the verses quoted were misquoted, and so rendered worthy of the epithet attached to them. This unpleasant discovery was presently followed by another—that the rudest most contemptuous personal remark was founded upon an ignorant misapprehension of the reviewer's own! And in ridicule of a mere misprint which happened to carry a comic suggestion on the face of it, the reviewer surpassed himself.

As Sefton read, Lufa laughed often and heartily; the thing was gamesomely, cleverly, almost brilliantly written. Annoyed as he was, Walter did not fail to note, however, that Sefton did not stop to let Lufa laugh, but read quietly on.

Suddenly she caught the paper from his hand, as quick as a kitten, saying, "I must see who the author of the precious book is!"

Her cousin did not interfere, but sat watching, almost solemnly.

"Ah, I thought so!" she cried, with a shriek of laughter.

"I thought so! I could hardly be mistaken! What *will* the poor fellow say to it! It will kill him!" She laughed immoderately. "I hope it will give him a lesson, however!" she went on. "It is most amusing to see how much he thinks of his own verses! He worships them! And then makes up for the idolatry by handling without mercy those of other people! It was he who so maltreated my poor first! I never saw anything so unfair in my life!"

Sefton said nothing, but looked grim.

"You should see—I will show it to you—the gorgeous copy of this same comical stuff he gave me today! I am so glad he is going—he won't be able to ask me how I like it, and I shan't have to tell a story! I'm sorry for him, though—truly! He is a very nice sort of boy, though *rather* presuming. I must find out who the writer of that review is, and get mamma to invite him! He is a host in himself! I don't think I ever read anything so clever—or more just!"

"Oh, then you have read the book?" spoke her cousin at length.

"No, but aren't those extracts enough? Don't they speak for themselves—for their silliness and sentimentality?"

"How would you like a book of yours judged by scraps chopped off anywhere, Lufa? Or chosen for the look they would have in the humorous frame of the critic's remarks? It is less than fair! I do not feel that I know in the least what sort of book this is. I only know that again and again, having happened to come afterwards upon a reviewed book itself, I have had to set down the reviewer as a knave, who for ends of his own did not scruple to make fools of his readers. I am ashamed, Lufa, that you should so accept everything as gospel against a man who believes you his friend!"

Walter's heart had been as water, but now it had turned to ice, and with the coldness came strength; he could bear anything except this desert of a woman. The moment Sefton had thus spoken, he rose and came forward—not so much to Sefton's surprise as Lufa's—and said, "Thank you, Mr. Sefton, for undeceiving me. I owe you, Lady Lufa, the debt of a deep distrust hereafter of poetic ladies."

"They will hardly be annihilated by it, Mr. Colman!" returned Lufa. "But, indeed, I did not know you were in the room; and perhaps you did not know that in our circle it is counted bad manners to listen!"

"I was foolishly paralyzed for a moment," said Walter, "as well as unprepared for the part you would take."

"I am very glad, Mr. Colman," said Sefton, "that you have had the opportunity of discovering the truth! My cousin well deserves the pillory in which I know you will not place her!"

"Lady Lufa needs fear nothing from me. I have some regard left for the idea of her—the thing she is not! If you will be kind, come and help me out of the house."

"There is no train tonight."

"I will wait at the station for the slow train."

"I cannot press you to stay an hour where you have been so treated, but—"

"It is high time I went!" said Walter—not without the dignity that endurance gives. "May I ask you to do one thing for me, Mr. Sefton?"

"Twenty things, if I can."

"Then please send my portmanteau after me."

With that he left the room, and went to his own, far on the way of being cured of his foolishness, though not quite so far as he imagined. The blood, however, was surging healthily through his veins; he had been made a fool of, but he would be a wiser man for it!

He had hardly closed his door when Sefton appeared.

"Can I help you?" he said.

"To pack my portmanteau? Did you ever pack your own?"

"Oftener than you, I suspect! I never had but one orderly I could bear about me, and he's dead, poor fellow. I shall see him again, though, I do trust, let believers in dirt say what they will. Never till I myself think no more will I cease hoping to see my old Archie again! But about Lufa and her kind—fellows must learn something through them, or they would make raving maniacs of us. God be thanked, He has her in His great idiot-cage, and will do something with her yet. May you and I be there to see when she comes out in her right mind!"

"Amen!" said Walter.

"And now, my dear fellow," said Sefton, "if you will listen to me, you will not go till tomorrow morning. No, I don't want you to stay to breakfast! You shall go by the early train as any other visitor might. The least scrap of a note to Lady Tremaine, and all will go without remark."

He waited in silence. Walter went on putting up his things. "I daresay you are right!" he said at length. "I will stay till the morning. But you will not ask me to go down again?"

"It would be a victory if you could!"

"Very well, I will. I am a fool, but this much less of a fool, that I know I am one."

Somehow Walter had a sense of relief. He began to dress, and spent some pains on the process. He felt sure Sefton would take care the *Onlooker* should not be seen—before his departure anyhow. During dinner he talked almost brilliantly, making Lufa open her eyes without knowing she did.

He retired at last to his room with very mingled feelings. There was the closing paragraph of the most interesting chapter of his life yet constructed! What was to follow?

Chapter 27.

A MIDNIGHT ENCOUNTER

Walter drew his table near the fire, and sat down to concoct a brief note of thanks and farewell to his hostess, informing her that he was compelled to leave in haste. He found it rather difficult, though what Lufa might tell her mother, he neither thought nor cared, if only he had his back to the house and his soul out of it. It was now the one place in the earth which he would sink in the abyss of forgetfulness.

He could not fashion the note to his mind, falling constantly into thought that led nowhere, and at last threw himself back in his chair, wearied with the emotions of the day. Under the soothing influence of the heat and the lambent motions of the flames, he fell into a condition which was not sleep, and as little was waking. His childhood crept back to him, with all the delights of the sacred time when home was the universe, and father and mother the divinities that filled it. A *something*, now vanished from his life, looked at him across a gulf of lapse, and said, "Am I likewise false? The present you desire to forget; you say, it were better it had never been. Do you wish I too had never been? Why else have you left my soul in the grave of oblivion?" Thus talking with his past, he fell asleep.

It could not have been but for a few minutes, though when he woke it seemed a century had passed, he had dreamed of so much! But something had happened! What was it? The fire was blazing as before, but he was chilled to the marrow! A wind seemed blowing upon him, cold as if it issued from the jaws of

109

the sepulchre! He linked the time to the night of Sefton's warning; was the ghost now really come? Had Sefton's presence then only saved him from her for the time? He sat bolt upright in his chair, listening, the same horror upon him as then. It seemed moments he thus sat motionless, but moments of fearful expectation are long drawn out; their nature is of centuries, not years. One thing was certain, and one only—that there was a wind, and a very cold one, blowing upon him. He stared at the door. It moved. It opened a little. A light tap followed. He could not speak. Then came a louder tap, and the spell was once more broken. He started to his feet, and with the courage of extreme terror, opened the door—not opened it a little, as if he feared an unwelcome human presence, but pulled it, with a sudden wide yawn, open as the grave!

There stood no bodiless soul, but soulless Lufa!

He stood aside, and invited her to enter. Little as he desired to see her, it was a relief that it was she and not an elderly lady in brown silk, through whose person you might thrust your hand without injury or offense.

As a reward of his promptitude in opening the door, he caught sight of Lady Tremaine disappearing in the corridor.

Lady Lufa walked in without a word, and Walter followed her, leaving the door wide open. She seated herself in the chair he had just left, and turned to him with a quiet, magisterial air, as if she sat on the seat of judgment.

"You had better shut the door," she said.

"I thought Lady Tremaine might wish to hear," answered Walter.

"Not at all. She only lighted me to the door."

"As you please," said Walter, and having done as she requested, returned, and stood before her.

"Will you not take a seat?" she said, in the tone of, "You may sit down."

"Your ladyship will excuse me!" he answered.

She gave a condescending motion to her pretty neck, and said, "I need hardly explain, Mr. Colman, why I have sought this interview. You must by this time be aware how peculiar, how unreasonable indeed your behavior was!"

"Pardon me! I do not see the necessity for a word on the matter. I leave by the first train in the morning!"

"I will not dwell on the rudeness of listening—"

"—to a review of my own book read by a friend!" interrupted Walter, with indignation. "In a drawing room where I sat right in front of you, and knew no reason why you should not see me! I did make a great mistake, but it was in trusting a lady who, an hour or two before, had offered to be my sister! How could I suspect she might speak of me in a way she would not like me to hear!"

Lady Lufa was not quite prepared for the tone he took. She had expected to find him easy to cow. Her object was to bring him into humble acceptance of the treatment against which he had rebelled, lest he should afterward avenge himself! She sat a moment in silence.

"Such ignorance of the ways of the world," she said, "is excusable in a poet—especially—"

"—in such a poet!" supplemented Walter, who found it difficult to keep his temper in face of her arrogance.

"But the world is made up of those that laugh and those that are laughed at."

"They change places, however, sometimes!" said Walter. This alarmed Lufa, though she did not show her anxiety.

"Certainly!" she replied. "Everybody laughs at everybody when he gets a chance! What is society but a club for mutual criticism? The business of its members is to pass judgment on each other! Why not take the accident, which seems so to annoy you, with the philosophy of a gentleman—like one of us? None of us heed what we say of each other! Everyone knows that all his friends pull him to pieces the moment he is out of sight, as heartily as they had just been assisting him to pull others to pieces. Every gathering is a temporary committee, composed of those who are present, and sitting upon those who are not present. Nobody dreams of courtesy extending beyond presence, and when that is over, obligation is over. Any such imaginary restriction would render society impossible. It is only the most inexperienced person who could suppose things going on in his absence the same as in his presence! It is I who ought to be pitied, not you! I am the loser, not you!"

Walter bowed and was silent. He did not see her drift. If his regard had been worth anything, she certainly had lost a good deal, but, as it was, he did not understand how the loss could be of importance to her.

With sudden change of tone and expression she broke out, "Be generous, Walter! Forgive me. I will make any atonement you please, and never again speak of you as if you were not my brother."

"It is not of the least consequence how you speak of me now, Lady Lufa; I have had the good though painful fortune to learn your real feelings, and prefer the truth to the most agreeable deception. Your worst opinion of me I could have borne and loved you still; but there is nothing of you, no appearance of anything even, left to love! I know now that a woman may be sweet as Hybla honey, and false as an apple of Sodom!"

"Well, you *are* ungenerous! I hope there are not many in the world to whom one might confess a fault and not be forgiven. This is indeed humiliating!"

"I beg your pardon; I heard no confession!"

"I asked you to forgive me."

"For what?"

"For talking of you as I did."

"Which you justified as the custom of society!"

"I confess, then, that in your case I ought not to have done so."

"Then I forgive you; and we part in peace."

"Is that what you call forgiveness?"

"Is it not all that is required? Knowing now your true feeling toward me, I know that in this house I am a mistake. Nothing like a true relation exists, nothing more than the merest acquaintance can exist between us!"

"It is terrible to have such an enemy!"

"I do not understand you!"

"The match is not fair! Here stands poor me undefended, chained to the rock! There you lurk, behind the hedge, invisible, and taking every advantage! Do you think it fair?"

"I begin to understand! The objection did not seem to strike you while I was the person shot at! But still I fail to see your object. Please explain."

"You *must* know perfectly what I mean, Walter! I cannot but believe you too just to allow a personal misunderstanding to influence your public judgment! You gave your real unbiased opinion of my last book, and you are bound by that!"

"Is it possible," cried Walter, "that at last I understand you? That you should come to me on such an errand, Lady Lufa, reveals yet more your opinion of me! *Could* you believe me capable of such vileness as to take my revenge by abusing your work?"

"Ah, no! Promise me you will not."

"If such a promise were necessary, how could it set you at your ease? The man who could do such a thing would break every promise!"

"Then whatever rudeness is offered me in your journal, I shall take as springing from your resentment!"

"If you do, you will wrong me far worse than you have yet done. I shall not merely never review work of yours, I will never utter an opinion to any man."

"Thank you. So we part friends?"

"Conventionally."

She rose. He turned to the door and opened it. She passed from him, her head thrown back, her eyes looking poisonous, and let a gaze of contemptuous doubt rest on him for a moment. His eyes did not quail before hers.

She had left a taper burning on a slab outside the door. Walter had but half closed it behind her when she reappeared with the taper in one hand and the volume he had given her in the other. He took the book without a word, and again she went; but he had hardly thrown it on the hot coals when once more she appeared. I believe she had herself blown her taper out.

"Let me have a light, please," she said.

He took the taper from her hand, and turned to light it. She followed him into the room, and laid her hand on his arm.

"Walter," she said, "it was all because of Sefton! He does not like you, and can't bear me to like you! I am engaged to him. I ought to have told you!"

"I will congratulate him next time I see him!" said Walter.

"No, no!" she cried, looking at once angry and scared.

"I will not, then," answered Walter, "but allow me to say that I do not believe Sefton dislikes me. Anyhow, keep your mind at ease, pray. I shall certainly not in any way revenge myself."

She looked up in his eyes with a momentary glimmer of her old sweetness, said, "Thank you!" gently, and left the room.

Her last glance left a faint, sad sting in Walter's heart, and he began to think whether he had been too hard on her. In any case, the sooner he was out of the house the better! He must no more trifle with the girl than an alcoholic with the brandy bottle!

All the time of this last scene, the gorgeous book was frizzing and curling and cracking on the embers. Whether or not she saw it I cannot say, but she was followed all along the corridor with the smell of the burning leather, which got into some sleeping noses, and made their owners dream the house was on fire.

In the morning, Sefton woke him, helped him to dress, got him away in time, and went with him to the station. Not a word passed between them about Lufa.

All the way to London Walter pondered whether there could be any reality in what she had said about Sefton. Was it not possible that she might have imagined him jealous? Sefton's dislike of her treatment of him might to her have seemed displeasure at her familiarity with him! "And indeed," thought Walter, "there are few friends who care so much for any author, I suspect, as to be indignant with his reviewers!"

living for—though, in truth, his life was so much the more valuable now that Lufa was out of it. Occasionally his heart would grow very gentle toward her, and he would burrow for possible ways to her excuse. But his conclusion was ever the same. How could he forget that laugh of utter merriment and delight, when she found it was indeed himself under the castigation of such a mighty authority of literature? In his most melting mood, therefore, he could only pity her. But what would have become of him had she not thus unmasked herself? He would now be believing her the truest, best of women, with no fault but a coldness of which he had no right to complain, a coldness comforted by the extent of its freezing!

But there was far more to make London miserable to him, for he was now at last disgusted with his trade; this continuous feeding on the labor of others was no work for a gentleman! He began to find in it certain analogies which grew more and more unpleasant as he regarded them. He was sick also of his poetizing. True, the quality or value of what he had written was nowise in itself affected by its failure to meet acceptance. It had certainly not had fair play, but had been represented as it was not, its character lied away! But now that the blinding influence of their chief subject was removed, he saw the verses themselves to be of little worth. The soul of them was not a grand all-informing love, but his own small, self-seeking passion for a poor show of the loveable. No one could care for such verses, except indeed it were some dumb soul in love with a woman imaginably like the woman of their thin worship! Not a few were pretty, he allowed, and some were quaint—that is, they had curious old-flavored phrases and fantastic turns of thought. But throughout there was no revelation! They sparkled with the names of things in themselves beautiful; but whether these things were in general wisely or fairly used in his figures and similes and comparisons, he was now more than doubtful. He had put on his singing robes to whisper his secret love into the two great ears of the public, desiring not sympathy from love and truth, but recognition from fame and report! That he had not received it was better than he deserved.

Then, what a life was it thus to lie wallowing among the mushrooms of the press? To spend gifts which, whatever else they were, were divine, in publishing the tidings that many had

116

done ill, that others had done well, that he was amusing, and she was dull! Was it worth calling work, only because it was hard and dreary? His conscience, his taste, and his impulses all declined to back him in it any longer. They asked him what he was doing for the world, how many books had he guided men to read, by whose help they might steer their way through the shoals of life. He could count on the fingers of one hand the works he had heartily recommended. If he had but pointed out what was good in books otherwise poor, it would have been something! He had not found it easy to be at once clever, honest, and serviceable to his race; the press was but for the utterance of opinion, true or false, not for the education of thought. And why should such as he write books, who had nothing to tell men that could make them braver, stronger, purer, more loving, less selfish?

What next was to be done? His calling had vanished! It was not work worthy of a man, but was as contemptible as that of the parson to whom the church is a profession! He owed his landlady money—how was he to pay her? He must eat or how was he to work? There must be something honest for him to do! Was a man to do the wrong thing in order to do the right?

The true Walter was waking, beginning to see things as they were and not as men regarded them. He was tormented with doubts and fears of all kinds, high and low. But for the change in his father's circumstances, he would have asked his help, cleared off all his debts, and gone home at once. And had he been truer to his father, he would have known that such a decision would even now have rejoiced his father's heart.

He no longer had confidence enough to write on any social question. Of the books sent to him, he chose those as seemed worthiest of notice, but could not do much. He felt not merely a growing disinclination, but a growing incapacity for the work. How much the feeling may have been increased by the fact that his health was giving way, I cannot tell; but certainly the root of it was moral.

His funds began to fail his immediate necessities, and he was forced to pawn his watch; he would have sold it but that it had been his mother's, and was a gift from his father. Upon his return he met Harold Sullivan, who persuaded him to go with him to the theatre. There, just after the first act he caught sight of Lady Lufa in a box, with Sefton standing behind her. There was hardly a chance of their seeing him, and he regarded them at his ease, glad to see Sefton, and not sorry to see Lufa, for it was an opportunity of testing himself. He soon perceived that they held almost no communication with each other, but he was not surprised, knowing in how peculiar a relation they stood. Lufa was not looking unhappy—far from it; her countenance expressed absolute self-contentment, and in all parts of the house she was attracting attention, especially from the young men. Sefton's look was certainly not one of content, but it was as certainly not one of discontent. It suggested power waiting opportunity, strength quietly attendant upon—though hardly expectant of—the moment of activity. Walter imagined one watching a beloved cataleptic; till she came alive, what was to be done but wait? God has had more waiting than anyone else! Lufa was an iceberg that would not melt even in the warm southward sea, watched by a still volcano, whose fires were of no avail, for they could not reach her. Sparklingly pretty but not radiantly beautiful, she sat glancing, glittering, anything except glowing. A glow she could not even put on—she did not know what it was. Now and then a soft sadness would for a moment settle on Sefton's face, like the gray of a cloudy summer evening about to gather into a warm rain. But this was never when he looked at her; it was only when, without seeing, he thought about her. Hitherto Walter had not been capable of understanding the devotion, the quiet strength, the persistent purpose of the man; now he began to see into it and wonder. While a spark of hope lay alive in those ashes of disappointment that had often seemed as if they would make but a dust heap of his bosom, there he must remain, by the clean, cold hearth, swept and garnished, of the woman he loved—loved strangely, mysteriously, inexplicably, even to himself!

Walter sat gazing, and as he gazed, simultaneously the two became aware of his presence. A friendly smile spread over Sefton's face, but with quick perception he abstained from any movement that might seem to claim recognition. To Walter's wonder, Lufa, so perfectly self-contained, so unchangingly self-obedient, colored—faintly indeed, but plainly enough to the eyes of one so well used to the white roses of her countenance. She moved neither head nor person, only turned her eyes away

118

and seemed, like the dove for its foot, to seek some resting place for her vision.

The sight awoke in Walter the first unselfish resolve of his life. Would he not do anything—could he not do something—to bring those two together? The thought seemed even to himself almost foolish; but spiritual relations and potencies go far beyond intellectual ones, and a man must become a fool to be wise. Many a foolish thought, many an improbable idea, has proved itself seed-bearing fruit of the kingdom of heaven. A man may fail to effect, or be unable to set hand to, work he wishes to do, and be judged, as Browning says in his *Saul,* by what he would have done if he could. Only the *would* must be as true as a deed, for then it is a deed. The kingdom of heaven is for the dreamers of true dreams only!

Was there anything Walter could do to help the man gain the woman he had so faithfully helped Walter to lose? It was no plain task. The thing was not to enable him to marry her—that Sefton could have done long ago, might do any day without help from him. As she now was, she was no gain for any true man! But if he could help to open the eyes of the coldhearted, conceited, foolish girl, either to her own valuelessness as she was, or her worth as she might be, or again to the value, the eternal treasure of the heart she was turning from, she would then be a gift that in the giving grew worthy of such a man!

Here, however, came a different thought, bearing nevertheless in the same direction. It was very well to think of Lufa's behavior to Sefton; but what had Walter's been to Lufa? It may seem strange that the reflection had not come to him before; but in nothing are we slower than in discovering our own blame—and the slower that we are so quick to perceive or imagine what we perceive as the blame of others. The very fact that we see and heartily condemn the faults of others, we use, perhaps unconsciously, as an argument that we must be right ourselves. We must take heed not to judge with the idea that by condemning evil we clear ourselves and so escape judgment.

Walter's eyes were opened to see that he had done Lufa a great wrong; he had helped immensely to buttress and exalt her self-esteem. In his whole behavior toward her, had he not been far more anxious that he should please her than that she should be worthy? Had he not known that she was far more anxious to be accepted as a poet than to be admired as a woman? More anxious, indeed, to be accepted than to be worthy of acceptance—to be the thing she wished to be thought?

In that review which, in spite of his own soul, he had persuaded himself to publish, knowing it to be false, had he not actively, most unconsciously, and altogether selfishly, done her serious intellectual wrong, and heavy moral injury? Was he not bound to make what poor reparation might be possible? It mattered nothing that she did not desire any such reparation, or that she would look upon the attempt as another wrong in the affair—possibly as a pretense for the sake of insult, and the revenge of giving her the deepest possible pain. Having told her the lies, he must confess they were lies! Having given her the poison of falsehood, he must at least follow it with the only antidote, the truth! It was not his part to judge consequences, so long as a duty remained to be done. And what could be more a duty than to undeceive where he had deceived, especially where the deception was aggravating that worst of diseases, self-conceit, self-satisfaction, self-worship? It was doubtful whether she would read what he might write; but the fact that she did not trust him, that—notwithstanding his assurance—she would still be in fear of how he might depreciate her work in the eyes of the public, would, he thought, secure for him a reading. She might, when she had read far enough to see his drift, destroy the letter in disgust. That would be the loss of his labor, but he would have done what he could! He had begun to turn a new leaf, and here was a thing the new leaf required written!

As for Sefton, what better thing could he do for him than to make her think less of herself? Or, if that were impossible, at least to make her understand that other people did not think so much of her as she had been willingly led to believe? In wronging her he had wronged his friend as well, throwing obstacles in the way of his reception! He had wronged the truth itself!

When the play was over, and the crowd was dispersing, he found himself close to them on the pavement as they waited for their carriage. So near to Lufa was he that he could not help touching her dress. But what a change had passed on him! Not once did he wish her to look round and brighten when she saw him! Sefton, moved perhaps by that unknown power of presence, operating in bodily proximity, but savoring the spiritual, looked suddenly round and saw him. He smiled and did not speak, but, stretching out a quiet hand, sought his. Walter grasped it as if it was come to lift him from some evil doom. Neither spoke and Lufa did not know that hands had clasped in the swaying human flood.

Chapter 29.

A HARD LETTER

Having made up his mind, Walter set to work on the letter as soon as he reached home. He wrote and destroyed and rewrote, erased and substituted, until, as near as he could, he said what he intended. At least it should not be mistaken for what he did not intend, which is the main problem in writing.

My dear Lady Lufa,
    In part by means of the severe lesson I received through you, a great change has passed upon me. I am no longer able to think of myself as the important person I used to take myself for. It is startling to have one's eyes opened to see oneself as one is, but it very soon begins to make one glad; and the gladness, I find, goes on growing. One's nature is so elevated by being delivered from the honoring and valuing of that which is neither honorable nor valuable, that the seeming loss is annihilated by the essential gain; the being better makes up—infinitely makes up—for showing myself worse. I would millions of times rather know myself a fool than imagine myself a great poet. For to know oneself a fool is to begin to be wise; and I would be loyal among the sane, not royal among lunatics.
    But it was not to tell you this that I began to write. It was to confess a great wrong which I once did you; for I cannot rest, I cannot make it up with my conscience, until I have told you the truth. It may be you will dislike me more for confessing the wrong than for committing it—I cannot tell.

Yet it is my part to let you know it, and nonetheless my part that I must therein confess myself more weak and foolish than already I appear.

You will remember that you gave me a copy of your drama while I was at your house; that same night I wrote the review of it which appeared in the *Battery*. I am ashamed to have to confess that I had taken more champagne than I hope I ever shall again; and, irreverent as it must seem to mention the fact in such a connection, I was possessed almost to insanity with your beauty, and the graciousness of your behavior to me. Everything around me was pervaded with rose color and rose odor when, with my head and heart, my imagination and senses, my memory and hope full of yourself, I sat down to read your poem. I was like one in an opium dream. I saw everything in the glory of an everlasting sunset; every word I read, I heard in the tones of your voice. I received every thought that awoke through the radiant consciousness of your present beauty. If ever one being was possessed by another, I was that night possessed by you. In a mood like that of an opium dream, I wrote the criticism of your book.

But on the morning after writing it, I found I could so little enter into the feeling of it, that I could hardly believe I had actually written what lay before me. I took the poem again and scanned it most carefully, reading with a deep, anxious desire to justify the things I had set down. But I failed altogether. Even my love could not blind me enough to persuade me that what I had said was true, or that I should be other than false to print it. I had to put myself through a succession of special pleadings before I could quiet my conscience enough to let the thing go and tell its lies in the ears of the disciples of the *Battery*. I will show you how falsely I dealt. I said to myself that in the first place, one mood had as good a claim as another, with regard to the worth of what it produced; that the opinion of the night, when the imagination was awake, was more likely to be just with regard to the poem, than that of the cold, unpoetic day. I was wrong in taking it for granted that my moods had equal claims—and the worse wrong, that all the time I knew I was not behaving honestly. As a factor in one of the moods, I persisted in leaving out the champagne I had drunk, not to mention the time of the night and the glamour of your influence. The latter was still present the next morning, but could no longer blind me to believe what I would most gladly have believed. With the mood of the evening, my judgment was altered, whereas a true judgment is the same in all moods, inhabiting a region above mood.

In confession, a man must use plain words—I was a coward, a false friend, and a false man. I kept myself from seeing the fact plainly, though I should have looked it in the face with the intent of meeting what the truth might render necessary. Yet, knowing that I was acting falsely, I sent off the review, regardless of duty; and in the sole desire of pleasing you, I had printed as my opinion that which had never been my opinion, except during that one night of hallucination. I recognized it for an hallucination, for the oftener I read, the more convinced I was that I had given such an opinion as must stamp me out as the most incompetent or the falsest of critics.

Lady Lufa, there is nothing remarkable in your poem. It is nicely, correctly written, and in parts skillfully contrived; but had it been sent me among other books, and without indication of the author, I should certainly have thrown it aside as the attempt of a schoolgirl who, having more pocket money than was good for her, had been able to print it without asking her parents or guardians. You may say this judgment is the outcome of my loving fascination; yet I cannot but think that something in yourself will speak for me and tell you that I am speaking honestly. Mr. Sefton considers me worthy of belief; and I know myself worthier of belief than ever before—how much worthier than when I wrote that review! Then I loved you—selfishly; now I love the truth and would serve you, though I do not love you the same way as before.

Through the disappointment you caused me, my eyes have been opened to see the way in which I was going, and to turn from it, for I was on the path of falsehood. O Lady Lufa, let me speak! Forget my presumption; you bore with my folly—bear now with what is true, though it come from a foolish heart! What would it be to us, if we gained the praises of the whole world, and found afterwards they were of no value in the great universe into which we had passed? Let us be true, whatever becomes of it, and look the facts of things in the face!

If I am a poor creature, let me be content to know it, for have I not the joy that God can make me great? And is not the first step toward greatness to refuse to call that great which is not great, or to think myself great when I am small? Is it not an impassable bar to greatness for a man to imagine himself great when there is not in him one single element of greatness? Let us confess ourselves to be that which we cannot consent to remain! The confession of *not being* is the sole foundation for *becoming*. Self is a quicksand; God is the only rock. I have been learning a little.

Having thus far dared, why should I not go further and say one thing more which is burning within me! There was a time when I might have said it better in verse, but that time has gone by—to come again, I trust, when I have that to say which is worth saying; when I shall be true enough to help my fellows to be true. The calling of a poet, if it be a calling, must come from heaven. To be bred to a thing is to have the ears closed to any call.

There is a man I know who forever sits watching, as one might watch at evening for the first star to come creeping out of the infinite heaven; but it is for a higher and lovelier star this man watches. He is waiting for a woman, for the first dawn of her soul. He knows well the spot where the star of his hope must appear, the spot where, out of the vast unknown, she must open her shining eyes that he may love her. But alas, she will not arise and shine. He believes, or at least hopes, that his star is on the way, and what can he do but wait? He is laden with the burden of a wealth given him to give—the love of a true heart—the rarest and the most precious thing on the face of this half-baked brick of a world. It was easy for me to love you, Lady Lufa, while I took that for granted in you which did not yet exist in myself! But he knows the truth of you, and yet loves.

Lady Lufa, you are not true! If you do not know it, it is because you will not know it, lest the sign of what you are should unenduringly urge you toward that which you will not choose to be. God is my witness; I speak in no poor anger, no mean jealousy. Not a word I say is for myself. I am but begging you to be that which God who made you intended you to be. I would have the star shine through the cloud—shine on the heart of the watcher! The real Lufa lies hidden under a dusky garment of untruth; none but the eye of God can see through the lovely thing He made, out of which the false Lufa is smothering the life. When the beautiful child, the real Lufa, the thing you now know you are not but ought to be, walks out like an angel from a sepulchre, then will the heart of God, and the heart of George Sefton, rejoice with a great joy.

Think what the love of such a man is. It is your very self he loves; he loves like God, even before the real self has begun to reveal itself. It is not the beauty you show, but the beauty showing you, that he loves—the hidden self of your perfect idea. Outward beauty alone is not for the divine lover. Until the woman makes it real, it is but a show, and until she makes it true, she is herself a lie. It rests with you, Lady Lufa, to make your beauty a truth, that is, a divine fact.

For myself, I have been but a false poet—a mask among poets, a builder with hay and stubble, babbling before I had words, singing before I had a song, without a ray of revelation from the world unseen, carving at clay instead of shaping it in the hope of marble. I am humbler now, and trust the divine humility has begun to work out mine. Of all things, I would be true and pretend nothing.

Lady Lufa, if a woman's shadow came out of her mirror and went about the world pretending to be herself and deceiving the eyes of men, that figure, thus walking the world and stealing hearts, would be you. Would to God I could exorcise that ghost of you, could say, "Go back, forsake your seeming, false image of the true, the lovely Lufa that God made! You are but her unmaking! Get back into the mirror; live but in the land of shows; leave the true Lufa to wake from the swoon into which you have cast her; she must live and grow and become, till she is perfect in loveliness."

I shall know nothing of the fate of my words. I shall see you no more in this world, except it be as I saw you tonight, standing close to you in a crowd. The touch of your garment sent no thrill through me; you were to me as a walking shadow. But the man who loves you sees the sleeping beauty within you! His lips are silent, but his love speaks by the very silence of his lips. I shall soon—but what does it matter? If we are true, we shall meet someday, and have much to say. If we are not true, all we know is that falsehood must perish. For me, I will arise and go to my father and lie no more. I will be a man and live in the truth—to try, at least, so to live in the hope of one day being true.

Walter Colman

The writing of this letter was a great strain to Walter, but he felt much relieved when he posted it the next morning. How differently did he feel after that other lying, flattering utterance, with his half-sleeping conscience muttering and grumbling as it lay in the post box. He walked then full of pride and hope, in the midst of his dream of love and ambition; now he was poor and sad and bowed down, but the earth was a place that might be lived in notwithstanding! If only he could find some thoroughly honest work! He would now rather have his weakness and dejection with his humility, than ten times the false pride with which he paced the streets before.

But as he came home that night, he found himself far from well and altogether incapable of work. He was indeed ill, for he could neither eat nor sleep, nor take interest in anything. His friend Sullivan was shocked to see him look so pale and wild, and insisted he must go home. Walter said it might be but a passing attack, and it would be a pity to alarm them; he would wait a day or two. At length he felt so ill that one morning he did not get up. There was no one in the house who cared to nurse him; his landlady did little or nothing for him, beyond getting him the cup of tea he occasionally wanted. Sullivan was himself ill now, and for some days did not see or hear of him.

Thus Walter had such an experience of loneliness and desertion as he had never had before. But it was a purgatorial suffering, as he began to learn how insufficient he was for himself; how little self-sustaining power was in him. Not there was the fountain of life! Words that had been mere platitudes of theological commonplace began to show a golden root through their ancient mold. The time came back to him when father and mother bent anxiously over their child. He remembered how their love took from him all fear; how even pain seemed to melt in their presence, for they would see that the suffering went at the proper time. All gentle ministrations to his comfort, the moving of his pillows, the things cooked by his mother's own hands, her gold watch to play with—all came back, as if the tide of life had set in the other direction, and was fast drifting back into childhood.

What sleep he had was filled with alternate dreams of suffering and home-deliverance. He recalled how different Aunt Ann had been when he was ill; in his present isolation, her face looking in at his door would have been as that of an angel! And he knew that all the time his debts were increasing—when would he begin to pay them off? His mind wandered; and when Sullivan came at last, Walter was talking wildly, imagining himself to be the prodigal son in the parable.

Sullivan wrote at once to Mr. Colman.

Chapter 30.

A SUDDEN JOURNEY

It was afternoon when Sullivan's letter arrived, and Mr. Colman had already gone to a town some distance away, whence he would not return till the last train. The letter with the London postmark naturally drew the attention of Aunt Ann and Molly. The moment the eyes of the former fell on Harold's name in the corner, they blazed.

"The shameless fellow!" she cried. "Writing to beg another ten-pound note from my poor foolish brother!"

"I don't think that is it, aunt," returned Molly.

"And why not, pray? How should you know?"

"Mr. Sullivan has had plenty of work, and cannot need to borrow money. Why are you so suspicious, auntie?"

"I am not. I never was suspicious. You are a rude girl to say so! If it is not money, you may depend upon it, it is something worse!"

"What worse can you mean?" That morning she had had a strange and painful dream about Walter—that he lay in his coffin with a white cat across his face.

"That Walter has got into some scrape."

"Why should he not write himself, if it were so?"

"He is too much ashamed, and gets his friend to do it for him. I know the ways of young men!"

"Perhaps he is ill!" said Molly.

"Perhaps. It is long since I saw a letter from him! I am never allowed to read or hear one!"

"Can you wonder at that, when you are always abusing him?

If he were my son, I should take care you never saw a scrap of his writing! It makes me wild to hear those I love talked of as you talk of him—always with a sniff!"

"Love, indeed! Do you suppose no one loves him but you?"

"His father loves him dearly!"

"How dare you hint that I do not love him!"

"If yours is love, auntie, I wish I may never meet it where I've no chance of defending myself!"

Molly had a hot temper where her friends were concerned, though she herself would bear a good deal without retorting.

"There!" said Aunt Ann, giving her the letter. "Put that on the mantlepiece till he comes."

Molly took it, and gazed wistfully at it, as if to read it through the envelope.

"What if he *should* be ill, auntie?" she said, her dream lingering on her mind.

"What then? We must wait to know!"

"Father wouldn't mind if we just opened it to make sure it was not about Walter."

"Open my brother's letter! Goodness gracious, what next? Well, you *are* a girl! I should just like to see him after you had opened one of his letters!"

Miss Hancock had herself once done so—out of pure curiosity, though on another pretense. It was a letter, as it happened, which he would rather not have read himself than have had her read, for it contained thanks for a favor secretly done, and he was more angry than anyone had ever seen him. Molly remembered the occurrence, though she had been too young to have it explained to her. But Molly's idea of a father, and of Richard Colman as that father, was much grander than that of most children concerning fathers. There is indeed a much closer relation between some good men and any good child than there is between the far greater number of parents and their children.

She put the letter on the chimneypiece, and went to the dairy—but only to think about the letter. Her mind kept hovering about it where it stood on the chimneypiece, leaning against the vase with the bunch of silvery green honesty in it. What if Walter were ill? Her father would not be home till the last train, and there would be none to town before the slow train in the morning! He might be very ill and longing for someone to come to him—his father, of course. Her father was as reasonable as he was loving, and she was sure he would never be angry without reason. He was a man with whom one who loved him, and was not presuming, might take any honest liberty!

He could hardly be a good man with whom one must never take a liberty! A good man was not the man to stand on his dignity. To treat him as if he were was to treat him as those who cannot trust in God behave to Him! They call Him the Supreme Ruler, the Almighty, the Disposer of events, the Judge of the whole earth, and yet they would not presume to say, "Father, help Thy little child!" She would not wrong her father by not trusting him! She would open the letter, but she would not read one word more than was needful to know whether it came to say that Walter was ill! Why should Mr. Sullivan have put his name outside, except to make sure of it being attended to immediately?

She went back to the room where the letter lay. Her aunt was still there, and Molly was glad of it. The easiest way of letting her know, for she would not have done it without, was to let her see her do what she did! She went straight to the chimney, reached up, and took the letter.

"Leave that alone!" cried Miss Hancock. "I know what you are after! You want to give it to my brother and be the first to know what is in it. Put it back this moment!"

Molly stood with the letter in her hand. "You are mistaken, auntie," she said. "I am going to open it."

"You shall do nothing of the sort—not if I live!" she returned, and flew to take the letter from her.

But Molly was prepared for the attack, and was on the other side of the door before she could pounce.

She sped to her room, locked the door and read the letter, then went instantly for her bonnet and cloak. There was time to catch the last train! She enclosed the letter in another envelope, addressed it to her father, and wrote inside that she had opened it against the wish of her aunt, and was gone to nurse Walter. She took money from her drawer and returned to face her aunt.

"It is about Walter. He is very ill," she said. "I have resealed the letter for father, and written him it was I that opened it."

"Why such a fuss?" cried Aunt Ann. "You can tell him your impertinence just as well as write it! Oh, you've got your bonnet on! Going to run away in a fright at what you've done? Well, perhaps you'd better!"

"I am going to Walter."

"*Where?*"

"To London to Walter."

"You?"

"Yes, who else?"

"You shall not. I will go myself."

Molly knew too well how Walter felt toward his aunt to consent to this. She would doubtless behave kindly if she found him really ill, but she would hardly be a comfort to him!

"I shall be ready in one moment!" continued Miss Hancock. "There is plenty of time, and you can drive me to the station if you like. Richard shall not say I left the care of his son to a chit of a girl!"

Molly said nothing, but rushed to the stable. Nobody was there! She harnessed the horse and put him to the dogcart with her own hands, in terror lest her aunt should be ready before her.

She was driving from the yard when her aunt appeared in her Sunday best. "That's right!" she said, expecting Molly to pull up and take her in.

But Molly touched up her horse, and Aunt Ann was left standing. It was some time before she understood that the horse had not run away.

Molly left the dogcart at an inn next to the station, then told one of the railway porters, to whom her father was well known, to look out for him by the last train, and let him know where the cart was.

She boarded for London, and left home behind—for only a time.

As the train was approaching London, it stopped at a station where another train already stood, bound in the opposite direction. It began to move while hers stood, and Molly gazed out of her window at the other train, watching the faces that drifted by in a kind of phantasmagoric show. Then, in the farther corner of a third-class carriage near the end of the train, she caught sight of a huddled figure that reminded her of Walter.

A pale face was staring as if it saw nothing, but dreamed of something it could not see.

Molly jumped up and put her head out of the window, but her own train was now moving. If it had been Walter, there was no possibility of overtaking him. She was by no means sure, however, that it was he. The only way to know was to go on to her journey's end!

Chapter 31.

DOING AND DREAMING

Walter passed a very troubled night and was worse, though he thought himself better. Sullivan looked in to see him before going to the office, and said that he would come again in the evening. He did not tell him that he had written to his father.

Walter slept and woke and slept again. All the afternoon he was restless, as one who dreams without sleeping. The things presented to his mind, and seeming to be with him, were not those about him. Late in the afternoon, the fever abated a little, and he felt as one who wakes out of a dream. For a few minutes he lay staring into the room; then he rose and with difficulty dressed himself, one moment shivering, the next burning. He knew perfectly what he was doing, his mind possessed with an unappeasable longing and absolute determination to go *home*. The longing had been there all night and day, except when it was quieted by the shadowy comfort of his visions; his resolve came now with the first return of awareness of his present surroundings. Better to die at home, he said to himself, than recover in such a horrible place! On he went with his preparations, mechanical but methodical, till at last he put on his great-coat, took his rug, searched his purse, found enough to pay his way home, went softly down the stair, and stood in the street, a man lonely and feeble, but with a great joy of escape.

Happily a cab was just passing, and he was borne in safety, half asleep again after his exertions, to the station and a swift train bound for home.

It was a wet night but not very cold, and he did not suffer at first—in fact, was more comfortable than he had been in bed. He seemed to himself perfectly sane when he started, but of the latter half of his journey he remembered nothing connected; only fragments of it returned to him later as the remnants of a feverish dream.

The train arrived late in the dark night, at an hour when a conveyance was rarely to be had. He remembered nothing, however, of setting out to walk home, and little as to how he fared on the way. His dreaming memory gave him but a sense of climbing, climbing, with a cold wind buffeting him back, and bits of paper, which must have been snowflakes, beating in his face; he thought they were the shreds of the unsold copies of his book, torn to pieces by the angry publisher and sent swirling about his face in clouds to annoy him. After that came a great blank.

The same train had taken up Mr. Colman at a junction. The moment he descended, the porter addressed him with Molly's message. Surprised and uneasy, he was putting some anxious questions to the man, when Walter passed him. The night was still dark and cloudy with snow, the wind was coming in gusts, now and then fiercely, and the lamps were wildly struggling against being blown out; so that neither saw the other. Walter staggered away, and Richard set out for the inn, to recover the cart and drive home as fast as possible; there only could he get light on Molly's sudden departure for London! In her haste she had not left message enough. But he knew his son must be ill; nothing else could have caused it! He met with some delay at the inn, but at length was driving home as fast as he dared through the thick darkness of the rough ascent.

After a long struggle with the weather, he arrived home safely, roused the stableman to care for the horse, and hastened into the house. There he speedily learned the truth of his conjecture, and was greatly comforted that Molly had acted so promptly. Then he realized that by driving to another station some miles farther off, at which a luggage train stopped in the night, he could himself reach London a few hours earlier in the morning. He went again to the stable, and gave orders to have the horse well fed and ready in an hour. Then he tried to eat the supper his sister-in-law had prepared for him, but with small success. Every few minutes he rose, opened the door and looked out. It was a very dark morning, full of wind and snow.

By and by he could bear it no longer, and though he knew there was much time to spare, got up to go to the stable. The wind met him with an angry blast as he opened the door, and sharp pellets of keen snow stung him in the face. He had taken a lantern in his hand, but going with his head bent against the wind, he all but stumbled over a stone seat, where the family would sit by the door of a summer evening. As he recovered himself, the light of his lantern fell upon a figure huddled crouching upon the seat, but in the very act of tumbling from it. He caught it with one arm, set down the light, raised the figure's head, and knew his son even behind the worn, death-pale features and wandering eyes. Richard uttered one wailing groan which seemed to spend his life, gathered Walter to his chest, took him up like a child, and ran staggering to the house with him.

As he went he heard at his ear the murmured words, "Father, I have sinned . . . not worthy . . ."

His heart gave a great heave, but he uttered no second cry.

Chapter 32.

DUTIES AND DEFIANCE

Had it not been for that glimpse Molly had at the station, she would have been in misery indeed when, on arriving at Walter's lodging, and being told that he was ill in bed, she went up to his room, and could find him nowhere. The landlady had never heard him go out, and until she had searched the whole house, would not believe he was not somewhere in it.

Rather unwillingly, she allowed Molly to occupy his room for the night; and Molly, that she might start back by the first train, stretched herself in her clothes on the miserable little horsehair sofa. She would not sleep, and was not a little anxious about Walter traveling in such a condition; but for all that, she could not help laughing more than once or twice to think how Aunt Ann would crow over her—basely deserted, left standing in the yard in her Sunday clothes! It was to her care, after all, that Walter was given, not Molly's! But Molly had done her duty, and did not need to be told that we have nothing to do with consequences, only with what is right. So she waited patiently for the morning.

But what was she to do when she arrived home? Aunt Ann would have installed herself as nurse! It would not matter much while Walter was really ill, so long as Aunt Ann would be good to him! But when he began to be himself again—for that time Molly must look out and be ready!

Molly was at the station long before the train, and reached home at the earliest possible moment. She was received at the door by her father, who had been watching for her, and who told her everything—how and where Richard had found him; how he had huddled with his boy in his own bed to recover the warmth that was life; how Aunt Ann had bustled about like a noiseless steam engine, getting hot bricks and hot bottles and more blankets; how they thought Walter would yet die before the heat got to him. Even when Walter had begun to show a little life, he had moaned and murmured, and seemed to be going through a succession of painful events. First he had uttered a cry of disgust, then called out for his father; then he would be fighting the storm with a wild despair of ever reaching his father.

But Walter was alive, and Aunt Ann had already established herself by his side. She spoke now to Molly as if the girl had but the minute before left the room, vouchsafing not a single remark concerning Walter, and yielding her a position of service as narrow as she could contrive to make it. Molly did everything Aunt Ann desired without complaint, fetching and carrying for her as usual. She received no recognition from the half-conscious Walter.

If it had not been that Aunt Ann must have rest, Molly's ministering soul would have been sorely pinched and hampered; but when her aunt retired, she could do her part for the patient's peace. In a few days he had come to himself enough to know who was about him, and seemed to prefer Molly's nursing. To Aunt Ann this seemed very hard—and hard it would have been, but that, through all her kindness, Walter could not help foreseeing how she would treat him in the health to which she was doing her best to bring him back. He sorely dreaded the time when, strong enough to be tormented, but not able to lock his door against her, he would be at her mercy. But he cherished a hope that his father would interfere. If necessary he would appeal to him, and beg him to depose Aunt Ann and put sweet Molly in her stead!

One morning, after Molly had been sitting up the night with the invalid, she found Aunt Ann asleep at the breakfast table and roused her.

"His father is with him now," said Molly. "I think he is a little better; he slept more quietly."

"He'll do well enough!" grunted Aunt Ann. "There's no fear of *him!* He's not the sort to die early! This is what comes of letting young people have their own way! My brother will be wiser now! And so, I hope, will Walter! It shall not be my fault if he's not made to understand! Old or young wouldn't listen to me! Now perhaps, while they are smarting from the rod, it may be of use to speak!"

"Aunt," said Molly, with her heart in her throat, but determined, "please do not say anything to him for a long time yet; you might make him ill again! You do not know how he hates being talked at!"

"Don't you be afraid. I won't talk *at* him! He shall be well talked *to,* and straight!"

"He won't stand it any more, auntie! He's a man now, you know! And when a mere boy, he used to complain that you were always finding fault with him!"

"Hoity-toity! What next! The gentleman has the choice, has he, when to be found fault with and when not?"

"I give you fair warning," said Molly hurriedly, "that I will do what I can to prevent you!"

Aunt Ann was indignant. "You dare tell me, in my own—" she was going to say *house,* but corrected herself "—in my own home, where you live on the charity of—"

Molly interrupted her. "I shall ask my father," she said, "whether he wishes me to have such words from you. If he does, you shall say what you please to me. But as to Walter, I will ask nobody. Till he is able to take care of himself, I shall not let you plague him. I will fight you first!"

Molly rose, and her flashing eyes and determined mouth cowed her aunt in a flame of honest anger. Aunt Ann shut her jaws close, and looked the picture of disappointed postponement.

That instant came the voice of Mr. Colman. "Molly! Molly!"

"Yes, Richard!" answered Aunt Ann, rising.

But Molly was out of the door before her aunt was out of her chair.

Walter had asked where Molly was, and wanted to see her—the first wish of any sort he had expressed!

Chapter 33.

MOLLY'S WINGS

It was a sweet day in the first of the spring, and Walter lay with his head toward the window. The sun was shining into the room, with the tearful radiance of sorrows overlived and winter gone, when Molly entered. She was at once whelmed in the sunlight, so that she could see nothing, while Walter could almost have counted her eyelashes.

"Stand there, Molly!" he cried. "One moment! I want to look at you!"

"It is not fair!" returned Molly. "The sun is in my eyes. I am as blind as a bat!"

"I won't ask you, if you mind, Molly!" returned Walter.

In these days he had grown very gentle. He seemed to dread the least appearance of exaction.

"I will stand where you like, and as long as you like, Walter! Have you not consented to live a little longer with us? O Walter, you don't know what it was like when the doctor looked grave over you!"

Molly stood in the sun and Walter looked at her till his eyes were wearied with the brightness she reflected, and his heart made strong by the better brightness she radiated. For Molly was the very type of a creature born of the sun and ripened by his light and heat—a glowing fruit of the tree of life amid its healing foliage, all splendor and color and overflowing strength. Self-will is weakness, while the will to do right is strength; Molly willed the right thing and held to it. Hence it was that she was so gentle. She walked lightly over the carpet, because she could run up a hill like a hare. When she caught selfishness in her, she was down upon it with the knee and grasp of a giant. Strong is that man or woman whose eternal life subjects the individual liking to the perfect will, for such a man or woman is free.

Molly wore a daring dress of orange and red. Scarce a girl in London would have ventured to wear it; few girls would not have looked out of place in it; yet Molly was right. Like a dark-cored sunflower, she caught and kept the sun.

Having gazed at her in silence for a while, Walter said, "Come and sit by me, Molly. I want to tell you the dream I have been having."

She came at once, glad to get out of the sun. But she sat where he could still see her, and waited.

"I think I remember reaching the railway, Molly, but I remember nothing after that, until I thought I was in a coalpit, with a great roaring everywhere about me. I was shut up forever by an explosion, and the tumbling subterranean waters were coming nearer and nearer! They never reached me, but they were always coming! Suddenly someone took me by the arm and pulled me out of the pit. Then I was in the teeth of a snowstorm. My breath was very short, and I could hardly drag one foot up after the other. All at once there was an angel with wings by my side, and I knew it was Molly. I never wondered that she had wings. I only said to myself, 'How clever she must be to stow them away when she doesn't want them!' Up and up we toiled, and the way was very long. But when I got too tired, you stood before me, and I leaned against you, and you folded your wings about my head, and so I got breath to go on again. And I tried to say, 'How can you be so kind to me? I never was good to you!' "

"You dreamed quite wrong there, Walter!" interposed Molly. "You were always good to me—except, perhaps, when I asked you too many questions."

"Your questions were too wise for me, Molly! If I had been able to answer them, this trouble would never have come upon me. But I do wish I could tell you how delightful the dream was, even for all the wind and snow! I remember exactly how I felt, standing shadowed by your wings, and leaning against

141

you!"

Molly's face flushed, and a hazy look came into her eyes, but she did not turn them away.

He stopped and brooded on his dream. "But all at once," he resumed, "it went away in a chaos of coalpits and snowstorms, and eyes not like yours, Molly! I was tossed about for ages in heat and cold, in thirst and loathing, with now one and now another horrid draught held to my lips, thirst telling me to drink, and disgust making me dash it on the ground—only to have the draught back at my lips the next moment. Once I was a king sitting upon a great tarnished throne, dusty and worm-eaten, in a lofty room of state, the doors standing wide, and the spiders weaving webs across them, for nobody ever came in, and no sound shook the mote-filled air. On that throne I had to sit to all eternity, because I had said I was a poet and was not! I was a fellow that had stolen the poetry book of the universe, torn leaves from it, and pieced the words together so that only one could make sense of them—and she would not do it!

"Then this all vanished, and I was lying under a heap of dead on a battlefield. All above me had died doing their duty, and I lay at the bottom of the heap and could not die, because I had fought not for the right but for the glory of a soldier. I was full of shame, for I was not worthy to die! I was not permitted to give my life for the great cause for which the rest were dead. But one of the dead woke and turned and clasped me; and then I woke, and it was your arms about me, Molly! My head was leaning where it leaned when your wings were about me!"

By this time Molly was quietly weeping. "I wish I had wings, Walter, to flap from morning to night for you!" she said, laughing through her tears.

"You are always flapping them, Molly! Only nobody can see them except in a dream. There are many true things that cannot be seen with the naked eye! The eye must be clothed and in its right mind first!"

"Your poetry is beginning to come, Walter! I don't think it ever did before!" said Molly.

Walter gazed at her wonderingly; how grown his little Molly was! What a peace and strength shone from her countenance! She was a woman, girl, and child all in one! What a fire of life there was in this lady with the work-stained hands—so different

142

from the white, wax-doll ends to Lufa's arms! That one was of the cold and ice, of the white death and lies; here was the warm, live woman-truth. He would never more love any woman in the manner he had. Could that be a good thing which a creature like Lufa roused in him? Could that be true which had made him lie? If his love had been of the truth, would it not have known that she was not a live thing? True love would have known when it took in its arms a body without a soul, a material ghost!

Another time and another day came to Walter and Molly—it was a cold evening, and the wind howled about the house, but the fire was burning bright. Molly had been reading to Walter, but stopped for a moment.

Walter said, "I could not have imagined I should ever feel at home as I do now! I wonder why it is!"

"I think I could tell you!" said Molly.

"Tell me then."

"It is because you are beginning to know your father!"

"Beginning to know my father, Molly?"

"You never came right in sight of him till now. He has been the same always, but you could not see him!"

"Why couldn't I see him, wise woman?" said Walter.

"Because you were never your father's son till now," answered Molly. "O Walter, if you had heard Aunt Ann tell what a cry he gave when he found his boy on that cold bench, in the gusty dark of the winter morning! Half your father's heart is with your mother, and the other half with you! I did not know how a man could love till I saw his face as he stood over you once when he thought no one was near."

"Did he find me on the stone bench?"

"Yes, indeed! O Walter, I have known God better and loved Him more, since I have seen how your father loves you!"

Walter fell to thinking. He had, indeed, since he came to himself, loved his father as he had never loved him before; but he had not thought how he had been forgetting him. And herewith a gentle repentance began, which had a curing and healing effect on his spirit. Nor did the repentance leave him at his earthly father's door, but led him on to his Father in heaven.

The next day he said, "I know another thing that makes me

feel more at home—Aunt Ann never scolds at me now. True, she seldom comes near me, and I cannot say I want her to come! But just tell me, do you think she has been converted?"

"Not that I know of. The angels will have a bad time of it before they bring her to her knees—her real knees, I mean, not her church knees! For Aunt Ann to say she was wrong would imply a change I am incapable of imagining. Yet it must come, you know, else how is she to enter the kingdom of heaven?"

"What then makes her so considerate?"

"It's only that I've managed to make her afraid of me."

Chapter 34.

MOLLY'S WORDS

The days passed; week after week went up the hill and out of sight; the moon kept on changelessly changing; and at length Walter was well, though rather thin and white.

Molly saw that he was beginning to brood. She saw also, as clearly as if he had opened his mind to her, what troubled him—he must work, but what was his work to be?

Whatever he does, if he is not called to it, a man but takes it up "at his own hand, as the devil did sinning."

Molly was one of the wise women of the world, and thus thoughts grew for her first out of things, and not things out of thoughts. God's things come out of His thoughts, while our realities are God's thoughts made manifest in things. Out of them our thoughts must come, and then the things that come out of our thoughts will be real. Neither our own fancies nor the judgments of the world may be the ground of our theories or behavior. This, at least, was Molly's working theory of life. She saw plainly that her business, every day, every hour, every moment, was to order her way as He who had sent her into being would have her order it. While doing God's things, God's thoughts would come to her. God's things were better than man's thoughts, for are not man's best thoughts the discovery of thoughts hidden in God's things? As she obeyed Him, perhaps a day would come for her in which God would think directly into the mind of His child, without the intervention of things.

For Molly had made the one rational discovery—that life is to be lived not by helpless assent or aimless drifting, but by active cooperation with the Life that has said, "Live!" To her everything was part of a whole, which, with its parts, she was discovering by obedience to what she already knew. There is nothing so suited for developing even the common intellect as obedience, that is, duty done. Those who obey are soon wiser than all their lessons; while those who do not obey will lose even what knowledge they started with.

Molly was not prepared to attempt convincing Walter that the things that rose in men's minds, even in their best moods, were not necessarily a valuable commodity, but that their character depended on the soil whence they sprang. She believed, however, that she had it in her power to make him doubt his judgment in regard to the work of other people; and that might lead him to doubt his judgment of himself and the thoughts he made so much of.

One lovely summer evening in July, they were sitting together in the twilight, after a burial of the sun that had left great heaps of golden rubbish on the sides of his grave, in which little cherubs were busy dyeing their wings.

"Walter," said Molly, "do you remember the little story— quite a little story, and not very clever—that I read when you were ill, called 'Bootless Betty'?"

"I should think I do! I thought it one of the prettiest stories I had ever read, or heard read. Its fearless directness, without the least affectation of boldness, enchanted me. How one—clearly a woman whose grammar was nowise to be depended upon— should yet get so swiftly and unerringly at what she wanted to say, has remained ever since a wonder to me. But I have seen something like it before, probably by the same writer!"

"You may have seen the same review of it I saw: it was in your own paper."

"You don't mean you take in *The Field Battery*?"

"We did. Your father went for it himself, every week regularly. But we could not always be sure which things you had written."

Walter gave a sigh of distaste, but said nothing. The idea of that paper, as representing his mind to his father and Molly, was painful to him.

"I have it here. May I read it to you?"

"Well—I don't know—if you like. I can't say I care about reviews any more."

"Of course not! Nobody should. They are only thoughts about thoughts about things. But I want you to hear this!" pleaded Molly, drawing the paper from her pocket.

The review was short, but long enough to express much humorous contempt for the kind of thing of which it said this was a specimen. It showed no suspicion of the presence in it of the things Walter had just said he saw there.

But as Molly read, he stopped her. "There's nothing like that in the story! The statement is false!" he exclaimed.

"Not a doubt of it!" responded Molly, and went on.

But, arrested by a certain phrase, Walter presently stopped her again. "Molly," he said, seizing her hand, "is it any wonder I cannot bear the thought of touching that kind of work again? Have pity on me, Molly! It was I, myself, who wrote that review! I had forgotten all about it! I did not mean to lie, but I was not careful enough not to lie! I have been very unjust to someone!"

"You could learn her name, and how to find her from the publisher of the little book!" suggested Molly.

"I will find her, and make a humble apology. The evil, alas, is done; but I could—and will—write another notice quite different."

Molly burst into the merriest laugh.

"The apology is made, Walter, and the writer forgives you heartily! Oh, what fun! The story is mine! You needn't stare, as if you thought I couldn't do it! Think of the bad grammar! It was not a strong point at Miss Talebury's! Yes, Walter," she continued, talking like a child to a doll, "it was little Molly's first! And her big brother cut it all up into weeny weeny pieces for her! Poor Molly! But even then it was a great honor, you know, greater than ever she could have hoped for!"

Walter stared bewildered, hardly trusting his ears. Molly an authoress? In a small way it might be, but did God ever with anything begin it big? Here he was home again, defeated, to find the little bird he had left in the nest beautifully successful!

The lords of creation have a curious way of patronizing the beings they profess to worship. Man was made a little lower than the angels; he calls woman an angel, and then looks down upon her! Certainly, however, he has done his best to make her worthy of his condescension. But Walter had begun to learn humility, and no longer sought the chief place at the feast.

"Molly!" he said, in a low, wondering voice.

"Yes?" answered Molly.

"Forgive me, Molly. I am unworthy."

"I forgive you with all my heart, and love you for thinking it worthwhile to ask me."

"I am full of admiration for your story!"

"Why? It was not difficult."

Walter took her little hand and kissed it as if she had been a princess. Molly blushed, but did not take her hand from him. Walter might do what he liked with her ugly little hand! It was only to herself she called it ugly, however, not to Walter! Anyhow, she was wrong; her hand was a very pretty one. It was indeed a little spoiled with work, but it was gloved with honor! It were good for many a heart that its hand were so spoiled. Human feet get a little broadened when walked in; human hands get a little roughened with labor, but what does it matter? There are other hands and feet, after like pattern but better finished, in the making now, and to be ready by the time these are worn out, for all who have not shirked work.

Walter rose and went up the stair to his own room, a chamber in the roof and crowded with memories. There he sat down to think, and thinking led to something else. Molly, now alone in the garden, sat still and cried; for though it made her very glad to see him take it so humbly, it made her sad to give him pain. Yet not once did she wish she had not told him.

148

Chapter 35

MOLLY'S WISDOM

After a while, as Walter did not appear, Molly went up to find him: she was anxious he should know how heartily she valued his *real* opinion.

"I have a little poem here—if you can call it a poem—a few lines I wrote last Christmas. Would you mind looking at it, and telling me if it is anything?"

"So, my bird of paradise, you sing too?" said Walter.

"Very little. A friend to whom I sent it, took it, without asking me, to one of the magazines for children, but they wouldn't have it. Tell me if it is worth printing. Not that I want it printed—not a bit!"

"I am beginning to think, Molly, that anything you write must be worth printing! But I wonder that you should ask one who has proved himself so incompetent to give a true opinion, that even when he has expressed his real thought, he has been unable to defend it!"

"I shall always trust your opinion, Walter—only it must be an opinion; you gave a judgment then without having formed an opinion. Shall I read?"

"Yes, please, Molly. I never used to like having poetry read to me, but *you* can read poetry!"

"This is easy to read!" said Molly.

> See the countless angels hover!
> See the mother bending over!

See the shepherds, kings and cow!
What is Baby thinking now?

Oh, to think what Baby thinks
Would be worth all holy inks!

But He smiles such lovingness,
That I will not fear to guess!

"Father called; you would not come!
Here I am to take you home!

"For the Father feels the dearth
Of His children round His hearth—

"Wants them round and on His knee—
That's His throne for you and Me!"

Something lovely like to this
Surely lights that look of bliss!

Or if something else be there,
Then 'tis something yet more fair;

For within the Father's breast
Lies the whole world in its nest.

She ceased. Walter said nothing. His heart was full. What verses these were beside Lufa's works!

"You don't care for them!" said Molly, sadly, but with the sweetest smile. "It's not that I care so much about the poetry, but I do love what I thought the Baby might be thinking; it seems so true, so fit to be true!"

"The poetry is lovely also!" said Walter. "And one thing I am sure of—the Father will not take *me* on His knee, if I go on as I have been doing. You must let me see everything you write, or have written, Molly! Should you mind?"

"Surely not, Walter! We used to read everything we thought might be yours!"

"Oh, don't!" cried Walter. "I can't bear to think of the beastly

150

business! I beg your pardon, Molly, but I am ashamed of the thing. There was not one stroke of good in the whole affair!"

"I admit," said Molly, "that kind of thing is not real work, though it may well be hard enough! But all writing about books and authors is not that kind. A good book, like a true man, is well worth writing about by anyone who understands it. That is very different from making it one's business to sit in judgment on the work of others. The mental condition itself of habitual judgment is a false one. Such an attitude toward any book requiring thought, and worthy of thought, renders it impossible for the would-be judge to know what is in the book. If, on the other hand, the book is worth little or nothing, it is not worth writing about, and yet has a perfect claim to fair play. If we felt differently at different times about a book we know, how am I to know the right mood for doing justice to a new book?"

"I am afraid the object is to write, not to judge righteous judgment!"

"One whose object is to write, and with whom judgment is the mere pretext for writing, is a parasite, and very pitiful, because, being a man, he lives as a flea lives. You see, Walter, by becoming a critic, you have made us critical—your father and me! We have talked about these things ever since you took to the profession!"

"Trade, Molly!" said Walter, gruffly.

"A profession, at least, that is greater than its performance! But it has been to me an education. We got as many as we were able of the books you took pains with, and sometimes we could not help doubting whether you had seen the object of the writer. In one review you dwelt scornfully on the unscientific allusions, where the design of the book was perfectly served by those allusions, which were merely to illustrate what the author meant. Your social papers, too, were but criticism in another direction. We could not help fearing that your criticism would prove to be quicksand, swallowing your ability for original, individual work. Then there was one horrid book you reviewed!"

"Well, I did no harm there! I made it out horrid enough, surely!"

"I think you did harm. I, for one, should never have heard of the book, and nobody down here would, I believe, if you had not written about it! You advertised it! Let bad books lie unheard of. There is no injustice in leaving them alone."

Walter was silent. "I have no doubt," he said at length, "that you are out and out right, Molly! Where my work has not been useless, it has been bad!"

"I do not believe it has been always useless," returned Molly. "Do you know, for instance, what difference there was between your notices of the first and second books of one author—a lady with an odd name—I forget it? I have not seen the books, but I have the reviews. You must have helped her to improve!"

Walter gave a groan. "My sins are indeed finding me out!" he said. Then, after a pause, he resumed, "Molly, you can't help yourself—you've got to be my confessor! I am going to tell you an ugly fact—an absolute dishonesty!"

From beginning to end he told her the story of his involvement with Lufa and her books; how he had gotten the better of his conscience, persuading himself that he thought that which he did not think, and that a book was largely worthy, where at best it was worthy but in a low degree; how he had suffered and been punished; how he had loved her, and how his love came to a miserable and contemptible end. That it had indeed come to an end, Molly drew from the quiet way in which he spoke of it; and his account of the letter he had written to Lufa confirmed her conclusion.

How delighted she was to be so thoroughly trusted by him!

"I'm so glad, Walter!" she said.

"What are you glad of, Molly?"

"That you know one sort of girl, and are not so likely to take the next upon trust."

"We must take some things on trust, Molly, else we should never have anything."

"That is true, Walter; but we needn't without a question empty our pockets to the first beggar that comes! When you were at home last, I wondered whether the girl could be worthy of your love."

"What girl?" asked Walter, surprised.

"Why, that girl, of course!"

"But I never said anything!"

"Twenty times a day."

"What then made you doubt her worth?"

"That you cared less for your father."

"I am a brute, Molly! Did he feel it very much?"

"He always spoke to God about it, not to me. He never finds it easy to talk to his fellowman, but I always know when he is talking to God! May I tell your father what you have just told me, Walter? But of course not! You will tell him yourself."

"No, Molly. I would rather you should tell him. I want him to know, and would tell him myself, if you were not handy. Then, if he chooses, we can have a talk about it. But now, Molly, what am I to do?"

"You still feel as if you had a call to literature, Walter?"

"I have no pleasure in any other kind of work."

"Might not that be because you have not tried anything else?"

"I don't know. I am drawn to nothing else."

"Well, it seems to me that a man who would like to make a saddle must first have some pigskin to make it of! Have you any pigskin, Walter?"

"I see well enough what you mean."

"A man must want long leisure for thought before he can have any material for his literary power to work with. You could write a history, but could you write one *now*? Even for a biography, you would have to read and study for months—perhaps years. As to the social questions you have been treating, men generally change their opinions about such things when they know a little more—and who would utter his opinions, knowing he must by and by wish he had not uttered them?"

"No one; but unhappily everyone is cocksure of his opinion till he changes it—and then he is as sure as before till he changes it again!"

"Opinion is not sight, as your father says," answered Molly. Again a little pause followed.

"Well, Molly," resumed Walter, "how is that precious thing, leisure for thought, to be come by? Write reviews I will not! Write a history, I cannot. Write a poem I might, but they wouldn't buy enough copies of it to pay for the paper and printing. Write a novel I might, if I had time; but how to live, not to say how to think, while I was writing it? Perhaps I ought to be a tutor, or a schoolmaster!"

"Do you feel drawn to that, Walter?"

"I do not."

"And do you feel drawn to write?"

"I dare not say I have thoughts which demand expression; and yet somehow I want to write."

"And you say that some begin by writing what is of no value, but come to write things that are precious?"

"It is true."

"Then perhaps you have served your apprenticeship in worthless things, and the inclination to write comes now of precious things on their way, which you do not yet see or suspect, not to say know!"

"But many men and women have the impulse to write, who never write anything of much worth!"

Molly thought a while. "What if they yielded to the impulse before they ought? What if their eagerness to write, when they ought to have been doing something else, destroyed the call in them? That is perhaps the reason why there are so many dull preachers—that they begin to speak before they have anything to say!"

"Teaching would favor such learning!"

"It would tire your brain, and give you too much to do with books. You would learn chiefly from thoughts, and I stand up for *thoughts*, although I believe *things* must come first. And where would be your leisure?"

"You have something in your mind, Molly! I will do whatever you would have me!"

"No, Walter," exclaimed Molly, with a flush. "I will take no such promise! You will, I know, do what I say or anyone else may propose, if it appears to you right! But don't you think that, for the best work, a man ought to be independent of the work?"

"You would have your poet a rich man!"

"Just the contrary, Walter! A rich man is the most dependent of all—at least most rich men are. Take his riches, and what can he do for himself? He depends on his money. No; I would have the poet earn his bread by the sweat of his brow—with his hands feed his body, and with his heart and brain the hearts of his brothers and sisters. We have talked much about this, your father and I. The idea that a man who works with his hands is not a gentleman is the meanest, silliest article in the social creed of our country. He who would be a better gentleman than the

154

Carpenter of Nazareth is not worthy of Him who gave up His working, only to do better work for His brothers and sisters, and then He let the men and women, but mostly, I suspect, the women that loved Him, support Him! Thousands upon thousands of young men think it more gentlemanly to be clerks than carpenters; but, if I were a man, I would rather *make* anything than add up figures and copy stupid letters all day long! If I had brothers, I would ten times rather see them masons or carpenters or bookbinders or shoemakers, than have them doing what ought to be left for the weaker and more delicate!"

"Which do you want me to be, Molly—a carpenter or a shoemaker?"

"Neither, Walter, but a farmer. You don't want to be a finer gentleman than your father! Stay at home and help him and grow strong. Plough and cart, and do the work of a laboring man. Nature will be your mate in her own workshop!"

Molly was right. If Burns had but kept to his plough and his fields, to the birds and the beasts, to the storms and the sunshine, what greater store of good words could he have left behind! He was a free man while he lived by his labor among his own people. Ambition makes of gentlemen time-servers and paltry politicians; of the ploughman-poet it made an exciseman!

"What will then become of the leisure you want me to have, Molly?"

"Your father will see that you have it! In winter, which you say is the season for poetry, there will be plenty of time, and in summer there will be some. Not a stroke of your pen will have to go for a dinner or a pair of shoes! Thoughts born of the heaven and earth and the fountains of water will spring up in your soul and have time to ripen. If you find you are not wanted for an author, you will thank God you are not an author. What songs you would write then, Walter!"

He sat motionless most of the time. Now and then he would lift his head as if to speak, but he did not; and when Molly was silent, he rose and again went to his room. What passed there I need not say. Walter was a true man in that he was ready to become truer. What better thing could be said of any unfinished man?

Chapter 36.

THE LAST, BUT NOT THE END

It was the second spring since Walter had come home again, and Molly and Walter sat again in the twilit garden. Walter had just come home from his day's ploughing. He was now a broad-shouldered, lean, powerful, handsome fellow, with a rather slow step, but soldierly carriage. His hands were brown and mighty, and took a little more washing than before.

"My father does not seem quite himself!" he said to Molly.

"He has been a little depressed for a day or two," she answered.

"There's nothing wrong, is there, Molly?"

"No, nothing. It is only his spirits. They have never been good since your mother died. Even so, he declares himself the happiest man in the county, now you are home with us."

Walter was up earlier the next morning, and again at his work. A newborn wind blew on his face and sent the blood singing through his veins. If we could hear all the very finest and smallest of sounds, we might, perhaps, gather not only the mood but the character of a man, by listening to the music or the discord the river of his blood was making, as through countless channels it irrigated lungs and brain. Walter's that morning must have been weaving lovely harmonies! It was a fresh spring wind, the breath of the world reviving from its winter swoon.

His father had managed to pay Walter's debts and redeem his mother's watch; his hopes were high, and his imagination active. His horses were pulling strong; the plough was going free, turning over the furrow smooth and clean. He was one of the powers of nature at work for the harvest of the year; and was in obedient consent with the will that makes the world and all its summers and winters. He was a thinking, choosing, willing part of the living whole, in a vital fountain issuing from the heart of the Father of men. Work lay all about him, and he was doing the work. And Molly was at home, singing about hers. At night, when the sun was set, and his day's work done, he would go home to her and his father, to his room and his books and his writing.

But as he labored, his thought this day was most often of his father: he was trying to *make* something to cheer him. The eyes of the old man never lost their love, but when he forgot to smile, Molly looked grave, and Walter felt that a cloud was over the sun. They were a true family—when one member suffered, all the other members suffered with it.

So throughout the morning, as his horses pulled, and the earth opened, and the plough folded the furrow back, Walter thought, and made, and remembered; he had a gift for remembering completions, and forgetting the chips and rejected rubbish of the process. In the evening he carried home with him these verses:

> How shall he sing who has no song,
> He laugh who hath no mirth?
> Will strongest cannot wake a song!
> It is no use to strive or long
> To sing with them that have a song,
> And mirthless laugh with mirth!
> Though sad, he must confront the wrong,
> And for the right face any throng,
> Waiting, with patience sweet and strong,
> Until God's glory fills the earth;
> Then shall he sing who had no song,
> He laugh who had no mirth!
>
> Yea, if like barren rock thou sit
> Upon a land of dearth,
> Round which but phantom waters flit,

Of visionary birth—
Yet be thou still, and wait, wait long;
There comes a sea to drown the wrong,
His glory shall o'erwhelm the earth,
And thou, nor more a scathed rock,
Shalt start alive with gladsome shock,
Shalt a hand-clapping billow be,
And shout with the eternal sea!

To righteousness and love belong
The dance, the jubilance, the song!
For, lo, the right hath quelled the wrong,
And truth hath stilled the lying tongue!
For, lo, the glad God fills the earth,
And Love sits down by every hearth!
Now must thou sing because of song,
Now laugh because of mirth!

Molly read the verses, and rose to run with them to her father. But Walter caught and held her.

"Remember, Molly," he said, "I wrote it for my father; it is not my own feeling at the moment. For me, God *has* sent a wave of His glory over the earth; it has come swelling out of the deep sea of His thought, has caught me up, and is making me joyful as the morning. That wave is my love for you, Molly—is you, my Molly!"

She turned and kissed him, then ran to his father.

Richard, in turn, read the words, and kissed Molly. For in his heart he sang this song, "Blessed art thou among women! For thou hast given me a son of consolation!"

And then to Molly he said, "Let us go to Walter!"

158

Editor's Afterword.

It is only fitting that George MacDonald should write a book about a man who first longs for worldly fame as a poet, and then afterward comes to long for fame with God instead.

MacDonald's first privately published works were translations of German poetry; his first public work was a book-length poem. As a result, some in his generation came to hail him first as a poet and second as a writer of novels and fantasies. And those who have long continued to study and follow the man often refer to him as simply "our poet." But most in our generation know him first as a writer of fantasies for children and for adults; second as a writer of stirring but overlong novels for adults; third as the creator of a handful of dense but rich theological essays and sermons; and only fourth—if at all—as a poet. His collected poems are not in print, and have not been for many years.

Did MacDonald fail, then, as a poet? Only perhaps. If we have forgotten him as a poet, at least we continue to find him a storyteller with much to teach us about man, about God the Father, and about Jesus the elder Brother.

Home Again appeared in 1887, and was MacDonald's twenty-second novel for adults. Like most of his work, this book seems to be drawn from the lessons of his own long life. There may or may not have been a Lady Lufa in his past; more than a few of his biographers have postulated a broken romance for the winter of 1842–1843—a season in which the impoverished Mac-Donald served as a librarian or tutor in a remote Scottish castle.

He himself never explicitly referred to the episode, but turned to a similar setting again and again in his fiction. One can only wonder if Lufa, this petite dark-haired beauty with the sleeping soul, had her origin and prototype in a daughter of the laird of that unidentified castle.

And *Home Again* is rich with insights into the true source and purpose and process of all good poetry, all good writing, and all good criticism. MacDonald took great pains with his writing, and sometimes received great pains from the unlearned and unearned criticism heaped upon him. Yet he himself was a reviewer and critic—the kind of critic who loves and knows his subjects. He lectured upon Burns and Shakespeare, Tennyson and Wordsworth, Milton and Coleridge—not so much to expose their weaknesses but to illuminate their strengths. And he knew his limits; he wrote once that he would not lecture upon Dante at all, for the "best and worst of reasons"—that he was incapable of doing so.

If the criticism of fools is worth nothing, the praise of fools is worth nothing more—nothing, when neither critics nor praisers have established a relationship through their knowledge of the subject and the author. "How worthless then is fame," MacDonald wrote in the preface to his collection of Sir Phillip Sidney's works, "when of him whom they praise, the praisers are so ignorant."

And here too MacDonald depicts the war of values between the worldly and the otherworldly; how the world squanders and kills time as a cure for boredom, while the follower of Jesus knows that time is passing all too quickly and should be redeemed and spent wisely. For is not our use of our time one of the talents given to us to invest? some of us will have multiplied talents to surrender to our Lord, while others will have only dirt-crusted coins, for we cling to the treasures we have been given by hiding them in the earth.

In his constantly straitened circumstances, MacDonald had to write both for love and for money, and to use his time wisely both in loving obedience and out of necessity. He sometimes suffered from the pointed pens of critics, yet all the time he knew the true worth of man's praise. Blessings do not necessarily come to those who strive for and collect the praises of man. Blessed rather is the man who trades wisely with his skills and with his time! Unto such will the Master say, "Well done, good and faithful servant!" And that is the only praise that will endure, the only praise that will matter when the story of our present world is told and done.

Dan Hamilton
Indianapolis, Indiana
1988

Home Again.

Fiction From Victor Books.

George MacDonald

A Quiet Neighborhood
The Seaboard Parish
The Vicar's Daughter
The Shopkeeper's Daughter
The Last Castle
The Prodigal Apprentice
On Tangled Paths
Heather and Snow
The Elect Lady
Home Again

The Boyhood of Ranald Bannerman
The Genius of Willie MacMichael
The Wanderings of Clare Skymer

Cliff Schimmels

Winter Hunger
Rivals of Spring
Summer Winds
Rites of Autumn

Donna Fletcher Crow

Brandley's Search
To Be Worthy
A Gentle Calling
Something of Value

Robert Wise

The Pastors' Barracks
The Scrolls of Edessa